NEW FICTION FROM UPSTART EAGLE

THE WHITE BUFFALO

Kathleen Lignell graduated from the University of California at Berkeley. She received a fellowship from the National Endowment for the Arts in 1984 and won the 1986 Pablo Neruda Poetry Award from *Nimrod* Magazine. Author of *The Calamity Jane Poems*, she is a writer/editor and teaches literature at the University of Maine.

THE WHITE BUFFALO

Kathleen Lignell

UPSTART EAGLE PRESS

UPSTART EAGLE PRESS
P.O. Box 159
Orono, Maine
04473, U.S.A.

First published in the United States of America by
Upstart Eagle Press, 1988

Copyright   Kathleen Lignell, 1988
All rights reserved

LIBRARY OF CONGRESS CATALOGING IN PUBLICATION DATA
Lignell, Kathleen.
The white buffalo.
I. Title.
88-040343
ISBN 0-929778-00-6

Printed in the United States of America by
Furbush-Roberts Company, Bangor, Maine

Cover design and artwork by MaJo Keleshian

*For my mother and father,
and the buffalo in San Francisco's
Golden Gate Park who taught me
a thing or two.*

THE WHITE BUFFALO

Part One

1 The Herd

There was a blanket over the prairies, wooly, thick, and brown. They pulled it up over their cold shoulders and made themselves comfortable. They tricked it over a nearby cliff and the blanket piled higher and warmer. They felt good about their ingenuity.

An American scene, certainly. Sometimes they couldn't tell whether they wore clothes or were wrapped only in thick robes. Maybe they were changing into buffalos. In this wild state, they began to rely more on their noses than their eyes. They could smell their enemies in the grass. Excited by the least disturbance, they would sniff the earth, step back, bellow, and tear up the ground with their horns.

Under their thunderous footsteps the grass had the richness of a carpet. And they grazed barefooted in that dwelling place, the West.

They looked something like the "Mexican bull" Hernando Cortez pictured them in 1521 when he saw them for the first time in a menagerie kept by Montezuma, with a bunch on their back like a camel, their flanks dry, their tails large, and their necks covered with hair like a lion. Cloven feet and armed head. Not easy to look at, the great dark head, low and fearful-looking, made men coil and run.

Buffalos may seem invulnerable, but they are not really. In fact, they would never choose to live all alone by themselves somewhere. They are typical Taurus children: Earth, Fixed; Ruler, Venus. (For Taureans, security and structure are most important.) To interfere with this organized security provokes the retaliation of temper. In order to succeed with Taureans, one must always use persuasion and never force.

Taurus, practical and anchored, surely set. Now, that would characterize the American buffalo--his four feet firmly planted on the ground, the ears alert to each rustle in the grass, nose to the wind. For generations, they roamed free, bred, raised their families, and died.

* * * *

Something was bound to come of this. Day by day and year by the future was pushing West, and things could not always be the same, of course.

One day while enjoying the shade among the pines, cracking the dry branches as they broke through the woods, the herd saw something they took for a distant comet. The earth unfolded and the edge of the land receded. The sky was immense beyond comparison.

Then they began to see the outlines of an animal like themselves, but massive and white.

They looked together toward the mountains, and they saw this creature gathering up rain and grass and insects, and nuzzling against these things, and then climbing up on a small butte and casting everything into the sky, watching them rise and disappear into the clouds.

This apparition was really an old bison, a retired buffalo who had been tormented and chased into the Black Hills and holed up there month after month until death would not even take him. He had a sturdy heart, old friends somewhere, and a home on the range.

His hide was worth a lot, because it was white. Many old hunters had doubts that he really existed, but reports of the legendary figure persisted. Prairie Dog Dave had once hunted him with a gallon of formaldehyde, his gun, and ammunition. Like mirages on the plains, appearing and disappearing, other white bison turned up from time to time. All those white markings which came from rubbing against the chalk cliffs, or a brown buffalo might turn white by wallowing in dried, light-colored mud. Or milk cows, all white.

But the herd was not prepared for this sudden vision. Like anyone else they wanted instant answers like quick-cooking oats. Now, coming upon this face inescapably recognized as having been theirs once, a face they hardly knew they had lost until this moment--it was almost too much for a cud-chewing animal to comprehend.

Slowly they backed up into the trees, waiting and looking as far ahead of themselves as they could.

The powerful bodies strain against the future. Looking into the distance, this is what they see: the plains that shuddered, cried out, shook up and down for a moment. They could see that they were in this for keeps, moving back and forth across invisible borders, the tightened trigger pointed at the vulnerable spot behind the left shoulder. They were tough campaigners, but wintered in sheltered valleys where they could dig out grass from under the snow. Easy to track and slaughter. Sometimes they starved.

They were thunder, but softened their hoofs, then moved again with a kind of gigantic confidence and pushed on, scattering the snow, as if after the hardship of the season there would be a more gentle purpose, traveling single file beside a river.

One step, then another. The medicine men in their buffalo caps, the Cheyenne in battle with the bison as decoy and shield. Muskets fired as fast as arrows, then the repeating rifle and twice as many killed for food. A high price for robes, sacrificial; the horns, their heirlooms. They walked around the bloody cheek, in all this vast graveyard, no witness, no one to see.

The herd waited in the trees for a long time, trying to make sense of what they had seen. They were frightened and wanted to run. Nobody spoke. When they came out of the pines, the white buffalo had disappeared, and nobody was sure of anything. Someone remarked that the grass seemed greener. After a while someone else said he felt full even though he hadn't eaten for hours.

They drank upstream coming ever nearer and nearer to the Black Hills. Then they went up into them as if they were a supermarket. They found grass on the parking lot. When they had had their fill, they followed after each other, drinking from full canteens and poking a wide tongue at the world.

They ended up at a mountain tarn that reflected the shadow of a large tree. By this time the moon was up and beginning to join the tree in the shimmering water. So they formed a ring around the lake, their shaggy shoulders rubbing against each other as they lapped the water.

Yet how could they trust this tranquillity, this moment of truce? The winds could come up at any moment. Sometimes at night storms hit them so hard they would pile their bodies together in an effort to stay warm and not be carried off, pushing against each other for contact.

For now, they felt safe and reassured. Already there were men out there who could credit two hundred or more dead buffalo to their guns. Already Buffalo Bill had begun to make a name for himself. But tonight, away from this skin on history, the grass was wet and thick, and the water was fresh.

Like newborn children they awoke the next morning, anxious for life. A light mist was rising from the surface of the lake, and they all wore hoary beards. But there was something new here. This morning, in the mist, they felt as though their breath were escaping out of their bodies. Something had changed, and this chill was creeping into their bones.

"Let's turn back and graze somewhere else," said one old-timer. Some were even ready to run.

Standing together under the dripping branches, a shiver ran through them as if someone had set off a line of dominoes. In a mutual gesture they raised their heads; they smelled something on the wind.

As a rule, hoofed animals have poor eyesight, with little focusing power. Grazing, as they do, in the close confines of large herds, they had no need to evolve sharp vision. It is their keen sense of smell, the wind blowing across the open country, that alerts them to danger.

As children, they all learn this, that is, they know it from birth--that the eyes at the sides of the head preventing them from seeing straight ahead, the immense shoulder impossible to see over and behind, that these do not effect their ability to elude their enemies. Even crossing a river, they will catch the scent.

Now they were frightened and wanted to run, but could not. Something forceful, almost stubborn, that they barely perceived through their normal senses, kept them in these woods.

And they waited, watching the cumulus clouds, as they had in their childhood, drift across the sky in the shape of buffalos.

* * * *

The white buffalo emerged from the edge of the forest into the spotlight of morning sun, which streamed down on his back creating the effect of a single candle blazing in darkness. This bull was an extraordinarily fine animal. He had come through many battles unscathed, and no fighting scars or wounds marred his body. Vigor and alertness shone in his eyes, and the herd stepped back to give him plenty of room. He was now thirty-five years old and weighed 2,600 pounds.

Without bothering with formalities, he got right to the point. "It is a bad time for the buffalo," he said. "For as long as we have been here, we have wandered wherever we wanted, without being swept into the current of events. Now we must leave the old trails behind."

From the moment he began to speak, the herd knew they were in the presence of something powerful. From the horns to the muzzle, the hair was stark white, and his face was the ghost of all of them. But he belonged to none of them, and he never rested anywhere. His eyes were still full of the dust of distant stampedes, and his shaggy mane was stiff with age.

They recognized what he was, and what they were for: to roam the West, confronting events with the same persistence they always had, but to pursue, from now on, something else that could run faster and maybe even outdistance them. They moved aside for the white buffalo, forming a horseshoe around him.

"We have been happy here and seldom hungry, and red men and buffalo have lived together like relatives. There has been plenty for both of us."

He sighed, shaking his mane as lightly as the wind lifting the pine needles.

"But now the white man is making little islands for us and other little islands for the Indians--but it is still the same West, the one pushing up against the Rockies, then flattening out like a griddle cake crisscrossed by the Platte, the Missouri, and the Colorado. My father and grandfather died on this range. And it was home again for all of us when we found each stream, each lake, each new grazing spot. When I found the quilt with rosebuds on it lying across my bed, I knew I was still in the same place.

"Sometimes when I can't get to sleep at night, I go sit by this lake and look down into myself until there is nothing to feel, nothing to hear except fish turning over in their sleep. I see the minnows safely camouflaged in the eelgrass, I rinse my hoofs, I sleep.

"But because my hide is white, men have set a higher price on my head. My reputation is spreading like a wanted poster in every cow town. They think because I am old I will be easy game.

"I have been hunted with every weapon known to man: converted Army rifles, ordinary carbines, and arrows in my time," he told them. "Men know that the way to hunt me is to run me down, weaken me, trick me. And even so I have never been captured."

"I admit I was younger then. Still playing cat and mouse with the world. But I am still young enough to lead you." He snorted, "I'm as strong as an ox!"

For a moment the herd was very close to him, and each pair of eyes briefly met his own, which suddenly seemed old and glazed. Then he turned and looked out toward the distant range of hills. The others knew he could see things they couldn't.

A slip of paper was handed up to the white buffalo. His battle plan. He read it: "E pluribus unum."

2 On the Range

Matt and Rob Josephson in western Kansas created their own battle plan and were able to get rich quick by it.

Sunday, December 8, 1870
After washing up, Rob, Jim and me all went into the Indian village and saw the squaws tanning buffalo robes.

Monday, December 9, 1870
Today we skinned 35 buffalo between us. It was cold all day and windy at night. I killed 5 of the buffalo.

Tuesday, December 10, 1870
Although we had our first snowfall last night, it was warm today. We wounded some buffalo, but didn't get them. Instead we went turkey shooting.

Wednesday, December 11, 1870
We all went into the Indian camp to do some trading. Except for Teddy who went to Dodge with the head of the camp. We saw Indians eating lice.

Thursday, December 12, 1870
It was so cold we couldn't work. We hauled wood and went to the Yahoos camp at night and played cards.

The retired buffalo had stepped down from the podium and was retreating into the forest. They could hear him humming "Home on the Range." Then, suddenly, they were alone.

"How can it be?" a young calf asked no one in particular.

They were all wondering the same thing. Wasn't the West still wild, the grass free, and civilization only a word in Noah Webster's dictionary? What were they to these white men who hunted their flesh for food and left the bones to rot, or skinned their furs for lap robes and left the carcass for maggots? They wished they could stay forever in the Black Hills, away from the horror below on the frontier.

The lead bull called them together to line up, and they marched off single file, carrying their childhood like lunch pails at their sides.

They remembered the song the white buffalo was humming and plunged into a good-natured chorus, stepping smartly in time to the words.

In the distance, they thought they could hear an answer to their chorus--a familiar voice. Joining in the old song like a cermony, their faith in song-power was reaffirmed.

By the time they had come down out of the hills, the rain was pounding against their backs. The wind was blowing so hard, nobody could hear anybody else. Bewildered, the herd scattered in the four directions.

Nearby, four open wagons heaped with dead buffalo formed a circle at the base of the hills. Bill Cody, perched on his buckskin horse Brigham, was standing up in the stirrups with a pair of binoculars to his eyes. He shifted in the saddle and focused on the Black Hills behind him. Rumors of gold in these hills had been spreading from camp to camp. If there was anything up there but scraggly pines, low scrub brush, and buffalo grass, he could not see it as he adjusted the glasses to their highest power. But then, treasure was something you usually had to dig for, that did not show its face until you'd worn out your life hunting it down.

The sun was directly overhead and it was time for Bill and the others, who had been hired by the Union Pacific to suppply meat for the railroad camp, to return with their wagonloads. Like most days they had met their daily quota of twelve buffalos early.

After they returned to camp and had skinned the hides, Buffalo Bill sat down to clean Lucretia Borgia, his converted Army rifle.

"I am just a butcher, delivering the daily meat," he thought. "Each day, for the butcher who begins to build a world, the West begins."

After they returned to camp and had skinned the hides, Buffalo Bill sat down to clean Lucretia Borgia, his converted Army rifle.

"I am just a butcher, delivering the daily meat," he thought. "Each day, for the butcher who begins to build a world, the West begins."

He regretted that he had not yet seen a truly big herd, the blanket of two or three thousand shaggies men bragged of stretching over mile after mile of open land. He thought of the inexhaustible supply of animals providing meat and robes and fertilizer.

The young hunter climbed into a clean pair of jeans. He put on an old sweatshirt, a red kerchief around his neck, the fur-lined boots. He felt sleepy and curled up against his saddle on the ground and shut his eyes.

Now the ground swelled, thundering into a dense, almost solid, roar, into which the heart was locked. The hunter felt something unassuaged inside him, and asked "What's there?" Ahead of him the brown dustcloud rose into the sky like a tornado. The silence that followed was a rainbow of many colors and arched very low to the ground.

Bill woke, searching the horizon for the rainbow he thought was there. Of course, nothing was there but the stack of brown hides blocking out his view of the Black Hills.

Three hours later he was peeking over the shoulder of the camp cookie at the tattered pages of the *Buffalo Cook Book*. Bill and the cook wiled away the afternoon by swapping recipes and anecdotes about unforgettable meals of buffalo meat.

The cook and Bill then traded their favorite buffalo recipes. The cook confided his secret method for cooking buffalo hump rib, using the most tender and delicious cut. Then Cookie handed Bill the cookbook open to the diagram in the back. Bill pored over the page and memorized all of the vital parts.

Just as Bill was falling to sleep that night he remembered his dream and wished he could clear that up too. He recalled that day on the range--buffalos piled on top of each other. The tasty meat barbecued at camp that night. The fur robes stacked and waiting to be shipped back East. Each object isolated, dragged from its boundaries, relocated. And this tremor in the heart which no longer made sense.

3 A Twice-Told Tale

The white buffalo had also prepared himself for the next day, as for a journey. He had embarked on tomorrow as though for America.

Beneath him Omaha, Denver, Dodge City drifted past, with their unending line of telegraph poles. What a well-ordered world, laid out like a blue and green topographical map, with concentric circles pinpointing each park, each overnight campground. He could see where this was leading: a sectioned world, white men here in the open, red men reserved, buffalos preserved. Everything exposed and spread out, and the unrolled map ready to be forced to lie flat on the sureness of the earth's curve.

"I'm alone," he mused. The sunlight reflected off his white surface. A turn on the heel and the entire landscape changed. A hard light above the mineral earth. Beneath this thick wool, a warm and fragile flesh. He stepped back, lowering his shaggy head, and pawed the ground, then moved down the mountain.

Today, old bull, you will cross the plains with the power of a landlord.

The first thing he saw when he began his journey was a buffalo killed for sport, his severed head hanging in a tree.

Whirling around in anger and despair, he found himself in front of a shack made entirely of buffalo chips, except for the windows which were clear Saran-Wrap.

A tall, thin man, who looked hungry, stood on the front porch, whittling a bar of Ivory soap in the shape of a buffalo.

The white buffalo, not knowing what kind of man this was and wanting to be polite, wished him a cheery "Good Morning."

This man, who was a poacher, lived just outside the entrance to Yellowstone National Park, where buffalo hunting was against the law. He waited for buffalo to wander outside the park's boundaries, and when they did, he killed them. Then he would take the animals north into Livingston, Montana to a taxidermist who would mount the head, tan the hide, and ship them east. The meat wound up at the local butcher shop. In New York the going price for the mounted head was $100.

The white buffalo had also prepared himself for the next day, as for a journey. He had embarked on tomorrow as though for America.

Beneath him Omaha, Denver, Dodge City drifted past, with their unending line of telegraph poles. What a well-ordered world, laid out like a blue and green topographical map, with concentric circles pinpointing each park, each overnight campground. He could see where this was leading: a sectioned world, white men here in the open, red men reserved, buffalos preserved. Everything exposed and spread out, and the unrolled map ready to be forced to lie flat on the sureness of the earth's curve.

"I'm alone," he mused. The sunlight reflected off his white surface. A turn on the heel and the entire landscape changed. A hard light above the mineral earth. Beneath this thick wool, a warm and fragile flesh. He stepped back, lowering his shaggy head, and pawed the ground, then moved down the mountain.

Today, old bull, you will cross the plains with the power of a landlord.

The first thing he saw when he began his journey was a buffalo killed for sport, his severed head hanging in a tree.

Whirling around in anger and despair, he found himself in front of a shack made entirely of buffalo chips, except for the windows which were clear Saran-Wrap.

A tall, thin man, who looked hungry, stood on the front porch, whittling a bar of Ivory soap in the shape of a buffalo.

The white buffalo, not knowing what kind of man this was and wanting to be polite, wished him a cheery "Good Morning."

This man, who was a poacher, lived just outside the entrance to Yellowstone National Park, where buffalo hunting was against the law. He waited for buffalo to wander outside the park's boundaries, and when they did, he killed them. Then he would take the animals north into Livingston, Montana to a taxidermist who would mount the head, tan the hide, and ship them east. The meat wound up at the local butcher shop. In New York the going price for the mounted head was $100.

Now, the white buffalo did not know all of this, and determined to be pleasant and nonviolent, he asked the man if he knew the way to the overnight campground in Yellowstone Park.

When he had given the bull directions, the man thought to himself, "That tender hump and uncanny white hide will make me a fortune. I'll have to proceed cunningly to catch this old bull." For a little while he walked along with the buffalo, tossing out banalities about the pretty wildflowers growing everywhere. Once he even said, "I believe you aren't listening to a word I say. Why, you're walking along as though you were on your way to work and it's so delightful out here in the forest. Why don't you stop and rest a while?"

The white buffalo looked around and realized he'd been so deep in thought that he hadn't noticed the sun dancing on the ferns or the wild larkspur and morning glories growing everywhere. While he stood still, the poacher raced ahead to the campground where he changed into the uniform of a park ranger.

Finally the buffalo moved on. When he arrived at the campground and picked out a spot for the night, he was surprised to see the ranger already there to welcome him.

"Good morning," he bellowed, but received no answer.

He went up to the log the ranger was sitting on: hunched over, looking so strange with the visor of his cap pulled down over his eyes, sat the poacher trying not to be recognized. The buffalo regarded the ranger in silence for a few moments, and then remarked aloud:

"Why, Ranger, what thin fingers you have!"
"The better to manipulate with."
"Why, Ranger, what long ears you have!"

"The better to catch what passes by."
"Why, Ranger, what lean ribs you have!"
"The better to eat you with!"
Hardly were the words out then the poacher jumped off the log, spinning a lasso over his head, and chased the poor buffalo into the creek behind the campground.

By this time the buffalo was seeing red, and he lowered his head, bellowed, and tore up the creek bottom with his horns. Then he began to think up a plan that would put this poacher in his place.

Meanwhile the man sneaked back and forth along the bank, then finally hid behind a tree to wait until the animal would return to the campsite in the evening. Then he meant to creep after him and capture him in the dark.

It was all very simple. He tied and untied a neat clovehitch knot in the rope he carried. He made up a game of his own. It went like this: He couldn't chase after the bull. Too risky. He had to let him step into the rope trick. It was something to do with his mind. He thought the buffalo had none. All afternoon he tied and untied knots, behind his back, blindfolded, standing on his head. It got so the rope was a part of his hand, grabby and sly. He could catch anything with this tricky rope of his.

A little ways up from the campsite was an outhouse with its door open waiting for someone. Just as the sun was beginning to slip down behind the mountains, the white buffalo made a run for it. Up the rocky creek bank, crashing through the trees, and thorugh the open door, slamming it violently behind him.

The crash woke the nodding poacher, and he took off after the bull in a flash. In one swift moment it was all over. He plunged through the door, with his lasso twirling, ready to snare the dumb animal, who was not so dumb. The buffalo, balanced on the shaky timbers of the outhouse ceiling, stuck out his left front hoof and kicked the thin man down the hole and then quickly slammed the cover back down on the wooden seat again. He shut the outhouse door tight on his expertise.

A green truck went by. It was the real ranger, driving through the campground in his National Park pickup. He slowed down when he heard the commotion across the creek. Then he saw the white buffalo looking sheepish in front of the outhouse door, and he called, "Come on out of there." The white buffalo scrambled up the bank and trotted over to the pickup, jumped over the tailgate into the back, and the ranger sped away.

Later that night the tall, thin man struggled out of his hole and walked home stinking and empty-handed to his house of buffalo chips.

Fairy tales have a way of coming true, and because of this, the white buffalo, knowing a moral when he saw one, thought, "Never as long as I live will I ask a stranger for advice."

4 Rosebud

The buffalo, who had recovered his wits, was proud of this new teaching. In his youth, books like *The Buffalo Hunters* by Marie Sandoz or William T. Hornaday's "The Extermination of the American Bison," published in the Smithsonian Institution's *Annual Report* for 1887, failed to offer him a single answer capable of saving him from extinction. Not even James Freeman's edition of the *Prose and Poetry of the Livestock Industry*, published in Kansas City in 1905, could reveal any secrets of the trade that would prevent the annihilation of his race.

What light now radiated from this morning's awakening. Its brilliant answer was as easy as the sun coming up each day. Action was again possible and promised success; even dangerous undertakings could be risked without further hesitation. He would rely on his wits, be resourceful as an Indian who uses every shred of the deer and buffalo for his sustenance.

A house of buffalo chips, how clever! Mentally, he began to list the myriad uses of the buffalo, Red Cloud, a Sioux chief, once told a white man:

> "His meat sustained life: it was cut in strips and dried, it was chopped up and packed in skins, its tallow and grease were preserved--all for winter use; its bones afforded material for implements and weapons; its skull was preserved as great medicine; its hide furnished blankets, garments, boats, rope, and a warm and portable home; its hoofs produced glue; its sinews were used for bowstrings and a most excellent substitute for twine."

He walked on slowly, and the night drew close around his shoulders. The sky was low and almost pure black. The buffalo felt the world clinging to him as if he were its last chance. Everywhere nature waited to be plundered, and was descending on him to stop this nightmare. The disrupters of old rhythms, the unhungry consumers, killers of animals, this wretchedness they were responsible for--the running would finally end.

His eyes lit up like a computer, the data filtering rapidly through his brain. He thought, "We will build it up again from scratch."

What in his wandering about the West, what in retirement, had he learned? Slowly he advanced, boring his way through solid mountains. And then withdrawn, alone in the Black Hills for years, cleansed by the isolation as by the rain. But, on coming back from these travels, what sort of creature had he become? He resurfaced, fresher than childhood.

He had stayed on in the cold, lonely hills, his anger directed toward reprisal, his heart set on revenge. But he had found nothing consoling in his most desperate plot.

A white mansion among the pines, one window lighting up and then another. And he said, "Here is the frame we supported with our own ribs."

The white buffalo walked down one morning from Wyoming, following the Yellowstone River that was on its way to meet the Missouri in northern Montana. Past Old Faithful and bubbling mud holes, the Continental Divide, and up into Montana beyond the Bull Mountains and the Little Big Horn. Finally he came to a small creek with cold, fresh water that poured down the rocky ridges through a canyon dividing the mountains from the plains. He dropped his great head into a deep, clear pool just below where the boulders made the river sing in the rapids. He listened with delight and wanted to join the ripple and motion of the river.

He liked the name, too.

The Rosebud.

This was no ordinary mountain stream, but a river with a tale to tell and, later a memory to mourn. For now it was still chattering and gay, running its course. Sometimes it would attempt to be more articulate, lapping its waves against the bank in garbled syllables. The pure water would speak outright, telling what it knew and what it would make of itself.

5 The Slaughteryards

Rarely did men kill an old buffalo bull for food. What little meat he had on his bones was usually very tough, and although easy prey, even wolves would leave an old, stray bull alone when they could find younger, meatier ones. But sometimes slim pickings caused a hungry wolf to change his mind and tackle the lone bull.

When the white buffalo saw a pack of wolves nearby, with their heads down intent on a meal, he figured they had found a weak antelope or maybe a poor, lost calf who had wandered off from the herd.

The pack was so preoccupied with their catch, they never noticed the old bull come up close for a better view. He peered over the heads of the circle of snarling animals and saw another old buffalo bull like himself, but brown.

He had apparently put up a hard fight, but now it was nearly over for him. His eyes were entirely gone, his tongue was chewed half off, and the skin and flesh on his legs were torn to shreds. He was bleeding and trembling, unable even to bellow out his grief. Now blind and nearly destroyed, he would soon be covered by the weather and cold nights, like a seed, waiting to emerge some spring in another living body.

The white buffalo felt a bite on the heart. He felt as though he had stepped aside to watch someone's intimate secrets revealed.

He crushed the little slip of paper with his hoof and tossed the crumpled battle plan away. His yearning, his faith having died momentarily, he was like the man who came to church too late. The sermon was already over, and the flock was returning to the real world outside, without having heard a single word.

Running, running.

* * * *

In this famous sepia photograph of Charles Rath's buffalo hide yard in Dodge City, Rath is sitting on the pile of hides. The man in the white shirt is D.W. Auchutz, who ran the hide bailer for Rath.

The caption under the photograph reads: "During the peak of the buffalo slaughter in western Kansas, this yard handled as many as 80,000 hides at one time."

The name Auchutz sounds suspiciously like a place where men were once herded, their dead bodies picked clean of gold watches and jewelry and the fillings in their teeth.

* * * *

He had seen enough atrocities to last a lifetime, but there was one more place the white buffalo wanted to go before he returned to the Black Hills for a brief rest.

"Don't be afraid," he counseled himself. "No animal with the power that exists inside your hump can fear the hand that is raised against you. One bellow, one snort, and these men must be children again, this West will be as wide as it ever was."

But he knew that his power was somehow dimninished in the presence of men's inventions, their nets and traps and scheming minds. His mind was not narrow like theirs. He had not confined himself to thinking only in terms of what could be made of something already perfectly useful.

"I hope you get slaughtered," the voice of the recent past whispered in his ear. But the white bull ignored it, and set off directly to see for himself the slaughterhouses of Topeka.

Three hours later, as he neared Topeka, another voice spoke. "Wait here; don't go any further." At the city limits, still a different voice: "Come right in, we've been expecting you."

He heard the last two voices like the echo of someone's guilty conscience. With messages like that they could run the world. Topeka, this windy city, was to be his first conquest. Nobody's noose would capture him here.

And then, the inevitable discovery. An odor at first, the smell of burnt popcorn, he thought. No, burnt flesh. Once when he had passed too close to an open fire, he had accidentally seared a hole in the side of his leg, and the stench had been the same. But this time it was not just a scorched leg, but the removal of whole hides, singed off the back like a peeled tomato with the pulp exposed.

It had been his own choice, after all, to come here and now he was overcome by the grief that was his own making. For an instant he could see his carcass hanging on a meat rack alongside ten thousand others just like it.

Pawing the earth uncomfortably, he had no idea what to make of this new life that continued to go stale. In this city, outside the vast stretch of stockyards, out here in the irritating wind, he felt like a granite rock. He could not move from this frozen position, his four hoofs set squarely on the earth, just barely trembling. He could not turn his immobile head away from the stinking vision penetrating his brain. It was all he could do to prevent himself from bellowing like a helpless calf.

At last the paralysis wore off and the buffalo collapsed in exhaustion on the grass. For a long time, he couldn't form a single rational thought. Instead, he took in the scene before him.

To his right were the railroad tracks with a line of stock cars six blocks long. Out of the cars, an endless stream of animals were being prodded into pens. Everywhere men were jabbing, poking, dragging, and lassoing buffalos into a lethal reality. The buffalos were all smart enough to know they didn't want to go there, and they, in turn, were stamping their hoofs, tearing apart the cars with their horns, and snorting and lowering their heads as if they intended to charge.

The white buffalo closed his eyes, and saw them once again at home. He tried to imagine the West without civilized men, but the image wouldn't appear. When he opened his eyes, in the midst of all that neglect for life, he knew how closely he was linked to every living thing. Although he was unsure of the future, he was certain of life.

No words would ease the distress in his heart, however he was now able to put aside the hideous smell and the sight of his own flesh and blood lined up outside the meat packing houses.

He picked himself up off the grass and slowly walked away.

Lifting and lowering his hoofs, he moved into a brisk trot. Left front, left hind, right front, right rear, springing forward into bound flight. Both front hoofs, then both hind ones, and now he was galloping into a smooth, headlong run.

6 Running

A person who has seen a buffalo run will never forget it. Strange, but beautiful, rising and falling like the rolling hills. Other animals often joined the buffalos running across the plains. They were drawn to them, like men to the West.

Dynamos. They would run mile after mile without effort or decreasing speed. On and on, tenacious, enduring, persistent as the incomparable landscape.

Buffalo Bill Cody, having spirited the mail horse on its way, left Dodge, St. Louis, and Topeka whirling in little dustclouds behind him. Fargo, Dakota Territory, where he was due by sundown, had no reason to wire Topeka to see if he would be on time. Bill Cody was always ahead of schedule. Besides, there was a legend to perpetuate--the Pony Express was a world famous team of crack race horses and ace jockeys. Now he was on his final lap, coming into the home stretch.

A powerful west wind was hitting him in the face, whipping the reins against his jacket as he rode. As if he were the one who had to strain against the bit, time and history depending on the messages in his pouch.

To the west thunder clouds were piling up like a stack of skinned hides. And in the Black Hills ahead of him an opaque rain was drenching the dry grass. Just as Bill looked over at the downpour, he saw a brilliant rainbow arched above the hills, and the sky suddenly grew clear on the horizon.

Wanting to see this phenomenon at closer range, he drew in the reins and the horse's pace slackened. He took out his binoculars and looked towards the hills again, where the rainbow was now close to the ground. The curtain was up: only the main actor was missing.

He adjusted his glasses until they were fixed on infinity.

Then a dot on the horizon caught his eye, a flash on the side of the hills. It was throwing off reflections like a piece of metal. Gold, he guessed. Finally grounded, the rainbow struck the flashing object, and the sky exploded with a wonderful glow of many colors.

Bill's horse had now come to a complete standstill, and he got off and continued looking through the glasses until the light merged with the evening star. He was still watching when it joined the Pole Star too, and rose above the hills.

That night, for the first time in his career with the Pony Express, Bill Cody brought the mail in late.

* * * *

"The moon will be up soon," thought the white buffalo.

His cheeks were puffing in and out from running, and the wind had roughened his shaggy coat until it stood straight out from his body like an aura. Drops of rain and sweat trickled from his beard. He felt lucky to emerge from the frontier by the arched end of the rainbow, where the plains met the gently sloping hills.

Inside the colorful prism was a house filled with the light from many windows. He opened the door and, in the moonlight, he saw that everything was still the same as he had left it.

Gratefully, he rested his weary head against his legs, drawn up tight against his body like a fist.

Part Two

7 How the Buffalo Got His Hump

Torso of muscular attitudes admires his ability to use his ears from a distance.
He's on his guard.
His compliment, the other's suspicion.
His suspicion, the other's power.
"Your exquisite sense of hearing...but you aren't listening to a word I say."
You may not understand at once this traditional double talk, ignoring the ulterior motive: "We have come to bury you."
Mouth talking to nose, torso to ears.

* * * *

The herd came back stalwart, their nomadic souls keeping watch in the center of themselves. They had approached the unknown cow towns with tight-set jaws, well protected and well hoofed. They had battled, they had suffered, they had crossed the Missouri, the North Platte, and the Colorado.

In one town they had seen a woman find herself again and again at the same rack of winter coats, choosing one for herself.

She wondered why she was acquiring this coat she doesn't or didn't need. So warm and rich as a thick, wool blanket.

She was glad when the coat didn't fit.

The herd had been gone a long time, scattered in four directions, and now they were back together. Brought here by the urgent message from the white buffalo himself. In the huge amphitheater the roar of reunion was comforting. They were all here, the young calves who had grown into handsome cows and bulls, and the old buffalos grown older. They came, dressed in the same brown, nearly black, skins they had worn when they left. Like any reunion, they felt an intense impact of solidarity.

The white buffalo came on stage. In the years that had intervened since they had last seen him, he had changed. Although many years older, his forehead shone even brighter, his walk was quick as an excited child's, and his fur and mane had the texture of a spring lamb.

Like an animal who has shorn himself of all false comforts, all illusions, the white buffalo had gritted his teeth and taken a hard look at the worst.

They wanted to hear him speak of the heady thrills of action, of the roar of the stampede, to tell why to be happy they could no longer content themselves, like the others, with the mowing of grass on weekends. It was the white buffalo's turn to explain Darwin or to offer advice. He had explained to them before, while there was yet time, how much grass and water one could carry inside his belly and still run from a trapper or hunter without getting cramps or falling behind from fatigue. He had told them of secret passes and arroyos to use as last-ditch escape routes, even drawn them a map and had it copied for handy reference.

They nodded, but still they wondered if this was the urgent business. He spoke of his own boyhood, of the changes that had taken place, and then this...

He said he wanted to teach them the history of their hump, the vulnerable shoulder they each held high like a sacrifice.

All ears, for the first time they could hear the breath of knowledge.

Mouth talking to nose, torso to ears.

* * * *

How the Buffalo Got His Hump

Of course, the opening line is like a legend: Once upon a time the buffalo had no hump. He could still wallow in the mud or sleep on his back just as he pleased, without having to find a comfortable position for his hump.

When the buffalo entered the land of the first people, men were not eating animals; men were digging roots and collecting berries, for imitating animals was still in vogue. The buffalo was grazing in the man's backyard when he first began to feel a tingle at the back of his shoulder, which he mistook for a cowbird, which often rode astride his back and pecked at bothersome flies.

A man said to his wife, "Get some wood and build a fire." The people, who were nearly starved, thought if they built a fire they might feel less hungry.

The woman went into the backyard to gather firewood and saw the buffalo. He looked just like the reverse side of a nickel. Or a Union Pacific boxcar. One of his sides read UNITED STATES OF AMERICA and the other, E PLURIBUS UNUM. While he was singing, the buffalo said:
"Take me,
  I am powerful."
She took him and wrapped him up in her apron, and carried him back inside. Now she knew they would have food. She went to her husband and showed him the buffalo, and he said, "Wife, make medicine from this beast that we may have food." Then he called all the men, women, and children to the lodge and told them there was going to be medicine.

Then the woman rubbed tallow on the buffalo's back. He began to sing when she did it. He sang to the woman:
"Take me,
  I am powerful."
In legends the characters always say things twice for emphasis, and the buffalo was no exception.

Then she began to sing and dance, and all the people joined in. They made a noise like buffalo. Slowly the medicine began to work, and above the buffalo's shoulders a hump began to rise, a dough into which the people kneaded their hunger and sorrows, their love of the prairies, the rain and the cleansing wind, the wisdom from the morning star, and the power to grow. Until this great hump had become an emblem, a blood-linked totem honoring the claim to life.

And the buffalo said:
"Take me,
  I am meat."

The man cut off the hump rib, that tenderloin, and the people were happy now and had plenty of meat. Everyone now believed in the power of the hump. And from that day, the buffalo has carried his hump in his back pocket, next to his license to practice medicine.

8 Dodge City

After dismissing the reunion class at the amphitheater, the white buffalo boarded the five o'clock freight out to Dodge City.

The herd, meanwhile, had been moved to tears by the story of their hump, this manitou they carried around like a sacrifice. Like fellow conspirators, they winked at each other out of their new knowledge of the buffalo heart.

At first they couldn't believe it. But they soon grew used to their new identity. Like all Taurus natives, they took things seriously and almost at once assumed their role as healers.

They paced up and down like doctors consulting their patients. Each of their steps was charged with important medical decisions. They would have liked to cry out to each other for help. But their humps rose above them like beacons pointing toward the past, the future.

At last they got up to go.

Before the white buffalo left for Dodge City, he had given them instructions for their next task. He wanted them to check out records, files, anything that could turn up possible leads to their survival. They were supposed to track down military spies, and if it turned out they were the ones responsible for the death of thousands of innocent buffalos, then they would be punished; if not by them, then by the new breed.

With their medical license, the handy pocket reference, and the white buffalo's instructions snapped inside their knapsacks, they started down the mountain.

The west wind at their backs accompanied them:

> *This nation, this buffalo nation--*
> *The buffalos I, the buffalos I,*
> *I make the buffalos march around;*
> *I am related to the buffalos.*

* * * *

Dodge City was nothing fancy. Somebody had put up some false-front wooden buildings on Main Street between First and Second Avenues. There wasn't much behind the facades.

Dodge was known as "the cowboy capital," mainly because a cowboy could have a rip-roaring time in Dodge. Besides a general store, there were three dance halls, an opera house, and six saloons. In the Long Branch Saloon, much of Dodge's violent history was acted out. Under its ornate chandeliers, Doc Holiday once saved Wyatt Earp's life. Cockeyed Frank Loving, a celebrated faro dealer, once killed a gambler in a quick gunfight at the Long Branch.

Since the white buffalo arrived, he had seen the sights. He thundered up and down the wooden sidewalk, forcing folks to move aside.

The disguise was perfect.
Who would have guessed?
Wyatt Earp?

Nobody would ever see him, pulled down like a shade over his own features.

He wore a costume of a buffalo hunter in the West. He wore a quilted heart on his sleeve and little gold rifles embroidered on the collar of his blue denim shirt. He covered his hoofs in regulation army boots. And his horns were hidden under a cowboy hat. Of course, his buckskins had lots of fringe.

So as not to draw attention, the white buffalo moved into a modest little sod house five miles out of town, where Tom Nixon, who slew over two thousand buffalo in one month, once lived. The place was known as Buffalo City, because it had originally been a trading post built to serve the buffalo hunters.

As the buffalo stepped over the threshold, his legs felt heavy. For a moment he shut his eyes, his head still full of the long train ride and the chattering of the tracks. His shoulders quivered from the vibrations of the cattle car. Then, entering the house, he slowly lay down on his side.

He rested, yielding to his weariness and his dreams. The buffalo looked gravely at the four walls, the open door, and the train tracks fifteen feet away. All of them lifesize. Yet it all seemed unreal. These gestures he didn't understand, forever beginning, ending, beginning again. For one hundred years, the lone witness.

He looked up at the ceiling and thought, "I'm tired," as the same vision overtook him. A brown dustcloud falling on the radiant landscape. The cow towns and grazing lands alike. A mountain off to the left; to the right, red men sitting cross-legged in a circle, and covering them all a blanket as big as all outdoors. He was safely lodged here as in the massive, white house of his own body.

He woke up hungry, and decided to go into Dodge for dinner. He had heard earlier that The Far West, a restaurant named after some painting by a man named George Catlin, was a popular hangout. He decided to go there.

* * * *

The white buffalo was sitting in a dark, obscure corner of The Far West eating his vegetarian dinner. He was seated near the window and from there he could see the daily life of Dodge City, some small boys fighting in the dirt, pretty women holding up their long skirts as they rushed past, and cowboys tying up their horses on both sides of the muddy street. Outside his window he could see the men going about humanity.

The smell of whiskey was drifting in through the open window. The white buffalo continued eating. But his thoughts were interrupted by a sudden commotion coming from directly across the street at the Long Branch Saloon. The white buffalo wondered what was going on.

Inside the Long Branch sat Buffalo Bill, now a young hero at twenty-five, and Kit Carson, long-time friends. They were talking loudly, after too many whiskeys, and much to the annoyance of the other customers playing faro at nearby tables. Kit Carson was an intense man with a white mustache. He was the consummate frontiersman, who was often described as an "Injun-lover" by his enemies. He was the kind of man who could best be described as a hopeless idealist. Buffalo Bill Cody was young and brash and wore a mustache and a goatee and lots of fringe on his buckskins. He had just finished killing off 4,280 buffalo in eighteen months. His faithful gun Lucretia Borgia leaned against the chair beside him.

They plunged into their conversation as if it were a meal.

KIT CARSON: Yep, Bill, dogged if I ain't glad to be back in the West again. When President Grant called me to Washington fur them high-level talks, I didn't figger I'd be gone so long. Gimme a pull on your bottle. I got a turrible dry. Man gits a hankerin' after so much ridin'.

BUFFALO BILL: What's it all 'bout, Kit?

Across the street in The Far West the white buffalo perked up his ears.

KIT CARSON: It's risky doin's. Looks like we're in fur another Injun uprisin'. The President wanted to discuss it with me. I told him that it cain't be avoided no ways. Yep, a serious Injun war is 'bout to break out on the plains.

BUFFALO BILL: Seems to me we could avoid this someways. You figger the government's like to take a hand in this uprisin'?

KIT CARSON: No doubt. Look at facts, kid. We've taken everything from the Injuns. First their tribal lands, and then their sacred huntin' grounds. They're out there now, I'm bettin', holdin' council and smearin' war paint all over their bodies.

BUFFALO BILL: Well, there must be something we can do!

KIT CARSON: I reckon you really don't understand, do ya, boy? It's the buffler. We're slaughterin' their sacred buffler by the thousands and they ain't goin' to stand by and let it keep happenin' no more. They lost their land, and now their food. I reckon I can sure see their side of it, by God!

BUFFALO BILL: But it's *our* West now; those buffler belong to us. Don't that mean nothin'?

KIT CARSON: Plain horseshit, son! The buffler don't belong to no one. They's free as the plains. Ain't you never seen one of those old shaggies with his nose to the wind, lookin' forever like the Statue of Liberty with his head high and shinin' like a torch? They don't belong to no one but the West itself.

BUFFALO BILL: Well, you wanna know what I think 'bout it, Kit?

KIT CARSON: What's that, kid?

BUFFALO BILL: Injuns cain't do nothin' right; not a damn thing. And this buffler business just shows I'm right. What's so sacred cow 'bout a bunch of dumb buffler, anyways?

KIT CARSON: I reckon it's a man's own business what he thinks. But this uprisin' trouble is mighty risky, anyways you lay your sights. Maybe the Injuns and us could've been friends, but I don't think so. Ten years too late anyhow. Way I see it, we belong to different worlds. We're builders. While the Injuns are content to live jist like they always done. I figger Injuns think different from whites.

BUFFALO BILL: You mean they don't think. Goddam fools! Jist keep tryin' to stop our march of progress, that's their way of fun. Like I always says, the only way to deal with hostiles is with a rifle. (*Pats Lucretia Borgia on the butt*)

KIT CARSON: (*Musing*) It's the buffler. Reckon so. I'm sure the heart of this whole matter's with the buffler. Told the President as much too! He agreed with me, but figgered there weren't a damned thing he could do 'bout it.

BUFFALO BILL: Uh-huh.

KIT CARSON: Yep, another five year and there'll be nothin' but coarse fur, and that goin' fast too! The buffler's nigh gone now. Won't be even a goddam poor bull thirty years ahead.

BUFFALO BILL: Amen, and pass the bottle!

KIT CARSON: Bill, I swear sometimes you don't hear a word I'm sayin'. It's a fool thing!

BUFFALO BILL: Well, we done our part, didn't we? What the hell right them Injuns and buffler got anyways? Where you headin' now, Kit?

KIT CARSON: I'm gettin' old, kid. Time to sit back and recollect things. Yep, think I'll be headin' home now. What 'bout yurself, Bill?

BUFFALO BILL: Wisht you'd change your mind 'bout goin' back home. It'll be fat doin's up north, Kit. I'll be movin' on first thing in the mornin' to join General Custer in the Black Hills.

    A simple scrape of a chair reestablished the world. The buffalo looked around him at the dimly lit restaurant and out the window at the black night.
    He had a bad taste in his mouth, a hot flash. It suddenly spread across his hump as he bolted into the flawless, night air.

9 In Captivity

As much as anything else, the pesky mosquito is the symbol of the wilderness in this country, with its ruthless mouth sucking on the red blood of America.

Buffalos are not bothered by them, and most Indians are immune to their bite, slapping bear grease on their skin as extra protection. But the white man fought the mosquito like an unholy vampire. Mosquitos bothered the settlers, the bullwhackers, and the mountain men alike. All across the West men have cursed this nasty insect.

The white buffalo moved about the one-room sod house, listening to the whine of the lone mosquito which had followed him through the door. He wondered what there was about this monotonous buzzing that irritated men so much.

He thought, "Yes, it's really quite clear. We are all captives of ourselves, held down by one thing or another, like this insect, this fugitive, this madman buzzing his head off, all of us looking for the open door."

The faces of his friends rose before him in the dark room. He recognized the cow standing over there at the edge of the herd. He had loved her once, and now she was gone. The herd was the same as ever. He wanted to be recognized by them, as though in calling out his name, they might release him.

Slowly, the old familiar landscape began to rise around him like a prison. The Badlands of Dakota, the Rockies, and the Tetons circled around him. How many times had he crossed the frontier and felt he had missed something? There was so much still to see. And do. He pushed out the bars on his face and crawled through the hole he made. In front of him was the West where everything was possible, where all was solid and as enduring as history. He found himself watching over his old friends like a sheepdog.

But not one was aroused. His flight out of bondage could save no one but himself. This town here? Mere history. He wanted to leave again. Survival did not depend on the past. He would put his dreams and old friends behind him, become himself again. The others could wallow in self pity if they wished. There was that whine again. And now it began to bother him too, and he reached up a ruthless hoof and squashed the skeeter into the wall. He was pulling himself up out of the mud, into an animal of his own measure, his own creation. He laughed at having rejoined his shadow dancing on the moonlit wall.

* * * *

The white buffalo awoke with a shudder. He looked up into the unfriendly faces of four hide hunters from Dodge, who had recognized his face from the wanted poster, followed him home in the black night, and were now yanking on each of his four, startled hoofs.

The old bull, who had been so careful about covering his tracks, was stunned at his undoing.

"We kin prob'ly git more 'an two hundred bucks fur him easy, I reckon," one of them said to the others. They smelled bad, and the buffalo turned his head away.

"Aw, look, ya hurt his feelin's, Dave." No one else said anything.

There was nothing else to say. The men shackled his front and hind legs together and carried him out to the open wagon, tossing him in like a heap of shorn wool.

Something about their early morning presence blighted all words, bent meanings, and garbled thoughts like jumbled type. The buffalo sighed. It was not a sound of surrender, but the tense intake of breath of a taut animal before he strikes.

He watched the sun move behind a cloud, and wondered to himself if one day there would be nothing left of the buffalo except a spot on the ground, and if in their wildest greed these men wouldn't try to slaughter that too.

The men were now talking about taking the buffalo to Missouri to sell him to showmen. They considered there might be more money in that.

And then suddenly the wagon was bumping down the Santa Fe Trail back toward Dodge.

The buffalo, who had been so well sheltered by that white house and its living robe of earth, listened to the sounds of the West moving away from him as the wagon traveled along. Little by little, his face grew hard and red as he jangled the shackles on his limbs. In his mind he sniffed the ground, stepped back, and tore up the earth with his horns.

He did this several times, the supreme effort showing in his trembling frame. And on the third attempt, he freed himself. The manacles fell open onto the wooden floor.

When the wagon stopped just short of the city limits, and before the men could step down from the front of the cart, the buffalo made his escape. It was hours later, after he had left that city over fifty miles behind him, his heart still beating wildly in his ears, that he could safely admit to himself that everything was in order again.

His brimming heart saw the range, the distant hills, the few animals grazing nearby, everything more precious than water. He drank it all in and then lay down on the grass to sleep. He pulled the rosebud quilt up around his shoulders and felt the earth shudder beneath his tired body.

10 A Greed for Gold

Buffalo. Everywhere buffalo chips underfoot on the trail, but there was no buffalo in sight. The men hiked down from the trail where there was a shack made entirely of buffalo chips in the clearing.

The roof had caved in and the tenant apparently had moved on years ago. Buffalo grass was growing up through the open door and windows.

They sat down in the tall grass. Over there the creek was laughing its way into the larger Yellowstone River. Birds were coming up close for handouts. They were big blue jays with spring on their wings.

The men stood up and started on their way again. In the woods the heavy pine scent came up from under their boots. Each broken blade of grass, each stirring bush, held a message for those who could see it.

Everything smelled of buffalo. The trees were suddenly more eye than eyed, each needle reflecting wool and the sound of a hoof cracking off a low branch. But what smelled most like buffalo was the very earth itself. They reached down and ran their fingers through the rich soil. They thought of this fertile, dark brown, nearly black, earth as it filled their minds with dreams of conquest.

That day the herd crossed the Yellowstone. They were so close that their shadows fell across the hunters asleep in the sun.

During these years of private investigation, they had grown wise.

Now they had eyes at the back of their heads.

* * * *

One morning several white men walked into the Black HIlls and began to dig for gold. It was early spring. Six good months of easy picking still lay ahead of them before the first snowfall. All around them was treasure in the tall grass. Nearby there was the noise of buffalo in the pines, but they sought this other thing that glittered, yellow, malleable, and ductile. They craved it like the Golden Age where humans could imagine themselves ideally happy, prosperous, and innocent.

The rush was on, and men approached looking for everything they ever wanted. They found golden eagles, goldenseal, goldfinches, gold bugs, goldenrod, and a horde of other gold diggers. Some found the golden rule, while still others stumbled across the golden mean.

There was one man, whose fever pitched so high, he thought he saw the legendary Golden Fleece. He ran after it as hard as he could, but he gave up the chase after a short run when he saw it was only a buffalo calf, frisking in the warm spring sun.

* * * *

Dear Kit,

  Yr letter explains why I been seein' these agints from Dodge talking to Genral Custer up here in the Black Hills. I figgered they was tryin to get the inside story on the gold thieves in these parts. But now I see they's lookin fur the white buffler that's disguised as a buffler hunter. I reckon the fellas think he's hidin up here somewhere. Yr right bout the Injun uprisin too. Its sure comin fast. Any goddam mountain man tell you that. Don't look like we're goin git back the Black Hills from the Injuns neither. We're still barterin though, wisht us luck.
  Not much luck huntin buffler meat here. Might be they's trapped out. But we'll find em. Always have.
  Wisht you were here.
Yr friend Bill

Dear Kid--

  Glad to hear from ya and know ya got everything under control up in the Hills. I wisht I could join ya, but ya know, I kinda like sittin back and relaxin fur a change. The West's some spectacular place. I just sit here and look out inta forever. Makes a man at peace with hisself.

    I told ya from the beginnin it were the buffler that was behind it all. If only we coulda stopped when we was ahead. That's all it woulda took. But that's all behind us now. I reckon I don't know where none of this'll lead except to bad luck fur us all.

    Keep me posted on what's goin on in yr parts.

Yr old pal Kit Carson

* * * *

They had called him a dumb animal.

    This time, surely, he would blush and tears form at the base of his eyelids. But no. He smiled at their simplicity and moved on. He knew who was in this for keeps and what the stakes were. He knew that the autumn brought harvests which faded into winter.

    The white buffalo was suddenly so sure of his life. He drew his confident strength from the grass, the mountains, and the open range that somehow survived in spite of every hardship.

    He drew himself up into a monument and touched everything that lived. And everything he touched, he healed. Every twig that had broken off, the trampled grass, every rock overturned, he retstored to its original condition.

    Nothing was stirring as he walked on. Even the wind had died down to a peaceful murmur. A feeling of calm passed over him like a truce, the quiet that comes before surrender or defeat.

And yet he had found the spring which had revived him. Here, close by. The others who were out there now, rediscovering the meaning of things, walked beside him in his mind, where at last he found himself at home.

The white mansion, with all of its windows lit up, looked impressive among the pines. He peeked through the windows and looked down into himself once again. His ribs were Early American furniture, and his hump rose like a red brick chimney against the clear sky.

11 A Western Tourist Attraction

Grass, earth, and rain. The yard in back of the house promised them eternity, and the house itself was filled with hundreds of buffalo, grazing close to the barbed wire fence and busy putting the finishing touches on Bill Cody's amateur hour.

The buffalos were a Western tourist attraction. Two thousand can still be seen in Custer State Park, South Dakota, during visiting hours. Grazing close to the fence, like watchful landlords, they continue to believe property is sacred.

Everyone ignores the "No Trespassing" signs, however. They lean inside the fence as far as they can, and call, "Come here, you old buffalos."

The children ask their mothers if they can ride on the humps and call them camels, until the park ranger, wanting to clear things up, teaches them this song:

> *Joe, Joe, broke his toe,*
> *riding on a buffalo!*

An architect from Manhattan tries to coax an old bull close enough to pet him but he goes about it all wrong. So do the children who sing the song.

Purely by accident, a mother of one of the children finds the best way to make friends with a reserved buffalo. The buffalo range reminds her of a favorite old ditty she used to sing at camp when she was a girl. First she starts humming the tune, and then she remembers the words. In all, she sings four verses of "Home on the Range," and by the time she is finished, the whole herd is heading straight for her like homing pigeons.

The calves nuzzle against her knees, and one of the older bulls lets her pet his shaggy, brown head. She wants to touch that wondrous hump, but it is entirely out of her reach.

Later, she is amazed at herself for not having run away when she'd seen them coming towad her. After all, they were wild animals, and you never knew what a captive wild buffalo might do. All those horrifying stories about the bears in Yellowstone. No, you could never be too careful when it came to wild animals.

After a while she forgot all about the buffalo, and while preparing dinner, she would absentmindedly find herself singing along with her daughter:

> *Joe, Joe, broke his toe,*
> *riding on a buffalo!*

* * * *

The blanket was shrinking, and it no longer stretched as far as the eye could see. The West had changed, and the view from its hump on history was changing with it. For a brief moment, the white buffalo wondered if he ever should have come out of retirement. Immediately he was ashamed of himself for his weakness. After all these years, wasn't his heart still sturdy and his belief in Darwin even yet intact? He snorted, all alone in the silence. The sound rolled across the plains like thunder.

A few of the young calves had laughed at the white buffalo's disguise when they had seen him coming from miles off in the distance. They had ridiculed the buckskin fringes and the quilted heart he wore on his sleeve. But when he drew closer and they saw the gold embroidered rifles on his collar, a loud gunshot riddled their contempt with solid bullets.

Now the herd leaned toward the old bull in a display of uninterrupted respect. They had come together again for a rally of solidarity. For one day they would demonstrate their united purpose by an observance of the ritual act of rubbing.

There was nothing the buffalo liked to do better than roll on the ground or rub up against a tree, large boulder, or other hard object big enough to accommodate his hump.

When men moved onto the plains, they gave the buffalo even more things to rub against. The corner of a sod house was perfect for rubbing, as was the telegraph pole. In fact, the poles were such a rubbing delight that herds would come from hundreds of miles for a rubdown. Each day the buffalos would shake down miles of poles, and each day men would put them back up again. It was a battle of the fittest, as much as anything else.

The buffalos loved rubbing as men loved music, luxury. Rubbing was not constantly on their minds, but they liked to think of it while they were busy grazing or drinking spring water. They would look up from the business at hand from time to time, a glazed expression in their eyes, and smile at the memory of a particularly fond rubbing experience. They kept repeating: "There isn't time...no time."

Now there was finally time, because rubbing had begun to assume the importance it deserved. In terms of their survival as a race, it had taken on new meaning. Today they were gathered together to consecrate this act, to set it in its proper niche in history. The white buffalo was already in the middle of his "Great Plains Address," which he had scribbled hastily on the back of a wanted poster:

"...a new nation, dedicated to the proposition that all living things are created equal."

As he spoke the buffalos contined to rub against the telegraph poles, knocking down one after the other at the height of their pleasure.

"Now we are engaged in a great plains war, testing whether men or buffalos can long endure. We are met on a great battlefield of that war, and we are here to dedicate this range as the final resting place for those bulls who gave their lives to man's frontier.

"It is altogether sporting and proper that we should do this. But the brave bulls, living and slaughtered, who struggled here, have consecrated it far above our poor power to add or subtract.

"It is for us rather to be dedicated here to the unfinished work of our forefathers, and we resolve that this West shall have a new birth of buffalo which shall not perish from the plains."

The white buffalo's hump rose and fell in the rhythm of the speech, and when he had finished, the magnificent white hump was so full of the medicine working inside it like yeast that it had grown by two or three inches.

Nothing was changed, yet everything was changed. The healing process had been restored again. Time past and time future gathered in one place and melded together like the impact of history. The herd felt their humps tingling with the knowledge of what is. They wanted to set off right away to finish the job they had begun. The great white bull had become their aura, emanating strength, become the expression of life, pervasive and sweet as the aroma of fresh spring buffalo grass.

12   Blood Brothers

The rally had been a success. Simply in terms of numbers alone, the head count was 1,300 buffalo. As compared to the hundreds of thousands that once ranged the West, a mere thousand wasn't much. But it was all there was.

The white buffalo looked at the fallen line of telegraph poles, at their feeble attempt to march across the plains like men. Behind the unfamiliar, coded message they carried, he glimpsed a fifteen-year-old boy just stepping into adolescence, but whose rapid development betrays his apparent innocence. He would cast a spell: one day taking everything into his head and punching it back out in code, buttons flashing, till it hurt. And then who would bellow and let them be themselves again?

There were worse things. He knew that the West had put a charm on men, that no reasoning, no pleading, would distract them from their headlong path. They could ride out the Santa Fe Trail whenever they pleased, and swell with mock ownership and pride. His heart moaned at the mere suggestion. Though he resented them, often feared them, there was always something between buffalo and men that bound them close like undiscovered brothers. Now, vulnerable and fallible as man, the white bull was as solitary as a single pine tree in an enormous landscape of grass.

He thought: it's the easy pickings which attracts them. They hunt down one beautiful, living thing until it is gone, and then move on to the next. Why would they never love the West as it was: solid, vast, with plenty for everyone in its entirety? Was this inconsummate greed for the hump rib, the choice part, all that they loved? What the buffalo carried inside his hump, they couldn't have cared a nickel about.

* * * *

Red Cloud wasn't all that an Indian chief should be. Even the white men knew when he had sold himself for another feast of crackers and molasses. He was middle-aged and still ambitious, and it was whispered that the white men had captured his spirit in their big black image box.

Red Cloud posed for his picture on a stiff, horsehair sofa. He was overexposed, but the Sioux back home thought it was the spitting image.

It was better to hunt buffalo on the Powder River than eat wormy pork from Fort Laramie. Crazy Horse and Sitting Bull sometimes went into Laramie to defy treaties, but otherwise they all stayed home.

They watched their day begin on the Powder River as clearly as the surveyor measuring the hills for the railroad. It was now late in the morning, and they were growing tired of watching the course of the day lengthen into someone else's shadow.

The Sioux made an awkward stab at ownership. They attacked the surveyors and eight troops of cavalry. Five times, like fleas, the Indians bit the dust. The blood coming out of their wounds was white.

The surgeon told them he'd come from another war party on the Little Big Horn where he had seen General Custer's blood coming out red. Nobody thought this was strange, for Custer had ignored the ghost shirts the Indians were wearing. These magic shirts with bright-colored buffalos emblazoned on them were impervious to the white man's weapons, even his powerful Hotchkiss rifle.

The Sioux said goodbye to the surgeon and left in the afternoon for Canada. The surgeon set off in the opposite direction for America, a place he remembered in his mind.

The West was now the color of blood, not just the bright crimson that blood turns when it touches the air, but the blood that stirs under an old wound that has never really healed.

Buffalo hearts were bleeding all over the plains. They mingled with the Sioux and Blackfeet and Cheyenne and became blood brothers, flowing into one another.

For one moment the buffalo had faced this red tide. Then the wave crashed, and he wheeled and ran. He bellowed again and again, but no one heard him.

Finally he gathered the herd together and they set off, as if everything were business as usual, in search of a nearby river or creek.

It was a cheerless morning, clouds and wind alternating with rain and hail. General Nelson A. Miles' forces were also setting off to face the hostiles on the Rosebud. As they marched they gradually became aware of two long lines of cavalry in their rear moving toward them on either flank. Were these General Sturgis' troops, or the warriors of Sitting Bull in pursuit? Anxiously, they watched the looming troops until they were relieved to see they were only buffalo marching in single file, with all the regularity and precision of well-trained soldiers.

The buffalos knew the men would not pursue them. It was the beginning of the end. There was now human game, meaner and more reluctant to give up the West without a battle. While the Indians still used what little clout they had left, the buffalo had resorted to their wits. They took a certain grim pleasure in outsmarting men, although their schemes would backfire at times. Those who were left were still practical and anchored, surely set.

Cautiously they stepped in each other's tracks, following the white buffalo to join the Indians' cause at the end of the trail.

Many of the mighty warriors were dead. It was a time of defeat and lack of hope, and in such a time new religions are born. Or the rebirth of what was always there, under the skin.

Among the Indians and buffalo a bond was being sealed tight like an American nickel, one side with the Indian head inscribed with "Liberty" and the buffalo side reading "E Pluribus Unum." Together they sang:

> *The whole world is coming,*
> *A nation is coming, a nation is coming,*
> *The eagle has brought the message.*
> *The father says so, the father says so.*
> *Over the whole earth they are coming,*
> *The buffalo are coming,*
> *The buffalo are coming.*

Just as years before the white buffalo had stepped down from the Black HIlls out of retirement, it was now Sitting Bull, the greatest maker of medicine among the Sioux, who chose to come forth from his retirement near the Standing Rock agency, and join the new religion. Now, together, the two bulls were forming a more perfect union.

At a chance meeting between Buffalo Bill Cody and General Miles, Cody asked the general if he knew who was behind the religion. When he found out it was Sitting Bull, he asked the general, "How 'bout giving me an order for his arrest?"

"Why not? You've known the old rascal for years. He might even listen to you," answered the general.

Buffalo Bill then requisitioned a wagonload of candy to lure Sitting Bull, who had a notorious weakness for sweets.

Off went Bill Cody and with him the West he was about to turn upside down.

Part Three

13 A Cold Wind

> *A cold wind blew across the prairie when the last buffalo fell...a death wind for my people.*
> ---Sitting Bull, 1876

A good buffalo hunting rifle cost money.

A 2000-pound buffalo bull was killed with a rifle that cost between $100 to $150, not including the necessary telescope sight.

It was against the natural order of death for a buffalo to die by having its sacred hump shot full of holes.

It might have been all right for the buffalo to be trapped in an early snowfall and suddenly die of the ordeal, or to be caught by surprise by a hungry pack of wolves, his powerful torso attacked on all sides, sprawled helpless, and unable to disentangle himself from the voracious dogs.

There are also buffalos who die of old age and their white beards are handed down to their children as protective talismans.

But for a buffalo to die from a shot through the hump was a manufactured order of death, and eastern companies like Remington and Sharps were its death cry.

Frank H. Mayer purchased his first Sharps second-hand from Colonel Richard Irving Dodge. It was a practically new .40-90-420. Mayer thought it was a beautiful piece, with its imported walnut stock and its shiny blue 32-inch barrel. At $125, he considered it a bargain. He was proud of that first Sharps of his. It killed quicker than anything he'd ever owned before. After a year or two, with plenty of buffalo dollars in his jeans, he even talked himself into believing that he needed an extra rifle in reserve--so he bought two.

There's no mention in history of how the buffalo went into frantic spasms when severely wounded by a Sharps hunting rifle.

His body would shake like someone's teeth chattering in the cold. Only a rifle could produce a death rattle like that.

The gun that won the West.

The buffalo were lying very still now. All but 800 of them were gone. Sitting Bull thought they had all disappeared except the white bull, but he was wrong.

* * * *

The creative force, a flower, was also about to establish itself and take the shape of the West.

The way of the shaman, the sage and healer who influences through the example he sets by the wholeness of his life, was in full bloom.

One bullet was all it took. When he was thirty, Sitting Bull was lamed for life, but it never limited his activities.

Sioux of Sioux, aloof, uncompromising, and courageous, he performed the Sun Dance in June of 1876. From one hundred punctures in his arms and shoulders, a vision bled forth: white soldiers falling upside down from the sky, making war as they fell, and the Great Spirit caring for the red men on the earth.

The Battle of the Rosebud.

Bleeding heavily, a vision half-fulfilled. At the end of the fight, General George Crook was forced to retreat, with heavy losses. A thorn in the side, plucked, bruised buds, deflowered, yet a quilt on which this nation rests.

A blue shadow, the army itself, approached, entering into the sound of the ringing nickel until the blue shadow and the nickel could not be held apart any longer. There was no song big enough for them both to sing.

General Miles' troops wore heavy buffalo coats over their blue uniforms. The Indians, who fought as best they could against the powerful buffalo robe medicine, soon were down to hand to hand combat. A slaughter, by anyone's account--men, women, and children face down, their tents destroyed, their bodies plundered.

It was evening and the red glow on the horizon was no longer rosy.

When the army left, there was blood everywhere. Handcuffed together, Sitting Bull sat next to the white buffalo in the back of an open wagoin, and Buffalo Bill offered them candy. Both refused. Their hearts were already in their mouths. Buffalo Bill took a couple of pieces himself.

The white buffalo was not worried about being killed by the men in blue uniforms. He knew that only history could kill him--individual men could never make him forget who he was. He had an inviolable idea of himself; he had dared to imagine and determine who he was and was therefore indestructible.

Buffalo Bill did not know him, and yet the white buffalo could sense that it was his own identity he sought, and no white bull. The Indian and the buffalo sat side by side, their free spirits soaring inside them with the speed of life.

Sitting Bull grimaced, looking at the buffalo. The old Indian showed nothing more, accepting the humiliation and defeat as if he'd been expecting them. He jerked again at the irons wrapped securely around his wrists and the buffalo moved closer to him. When he'd pondered a while, he looked up into Sitting Bull's clouded, brown eyes.

"We could escape now if we wished," said the buffalo, shaking his white beard in disagreement with himself. "But I think we're safer staying where we are, letting them think we have finally given up."

Sitting Bull smiled a slight grin of approval at the buffalo's words. He himself had none to offer. He had done all he could, reached out, attacked, struck the living enemy, and then been captured. It was the way of his people to resist, to hold out to the end. At fourteen,

Sitting Bull had counted his first coup, and now numbering in the thousands, the enemy he touched had struck him back.

"Good shots, good riders, and the best fighters the sun ever shone on," General Benteen admitted about the Sioux.

Who could miss the grim parallel in history? The West had reluctantly changed hands, red and white and blue, separated like the yolks of eggs.

The white buffalo cocked his ears. Far away he heard the empty ring of a hollow, counterfeit nickel.

When they came out on the open plains, the blazing blue shadow loomed over the wagon until it seemed to be everywhere.

The white buffalo wanted to run, but he was pitifully tired and had already decided against it. He knew the power of his hump had become great medicine and would protect him from being slaughtered.

Buffalo Bill regarded the bull in silence, searching for something in the buffalo's eyes. He must not have found what he was looking for, because he seemed confused when he turned away. Bill Cody had never seen a white buffalo before.

He took no notice of Sitting Bull until the Indian chief cleared his throat and solemnly asked, "What do you plan to do with us, Bill?"

Then silence. Strange, the sight of a pale young man wearing out two bulls; a man who, with a buffalo-head goatee and a hatchet nose, was dragging them to the ends of the earth.

When the sun fell behind the Black Hills, the sky turned a deeper blue and the mosquitos began to swarm thicker than ever. Then a day came like destiny; the wild herds were gone, and with them the nomadic soul of the West.

A whole nation won't die, but whole camps did, and familes, and breeds.

Knowing the diminished herd would wait there like hidden fish in their crevices for him to return, the white buffalo began his enforced journey across the vast American sea.

He was curious about his trip and asked for an itinerary, but none was available.

First they stopped at Dodge City for fresh horses and supplies, and he remembered his stay there six months earlier and wondered whatever happened to the four hunters who smelled bad.

As they started on the road again, he experienced a deep reverie and recalled his childhood. Trees and plains--simple things. One day the child he once had been came to him to tell him he would always be there. Sure of himself, linked to every living thing, the white buffalo carried everything inside him like the pulse of the earth.

Dawn near Dodge City raised wave after wave of amber grain and immense skies above the plains. Scenery without a final horizon, stretching on and on as far as the eye could see.

The white buffalo and Sitting Bull could see the texture of the land shifting like sand, always the same but ever different. Underneath the top soil was the Western world, permanent and virile.

Many weeks later they stopped again while Colonel William Cody was awarded the highest military citation, the Medal of Honor for bravery in action against Indians.

Another black nightmare was ending, totally unexpected and frightful. The old bull and the Indian sat in the back of the wagon, victims of the invention of the wheel, this cycle, vicious and without end. For a few hours the naked earth had exposed its perfect body to them, and now they were prisoners again, caught up in this world of words, crumbling slowly into narrow highways.

Nobody had told the two prisoners that at this ceremony Bill had also announced his retirement from the army.

On his way to stardom, William Cody dropped off his two prisoners of war at the Leavenworth penitentiary, then he wound his way into the heart of the American dream.

14 Buffalo Bill's Wild West Show

Buffalo Bill's Wild West Show appeared suddenly out of nowhere, arriving on Broadway in a magnificent, stainless-steel boxcar from Kansas. Emblazoned on one side were the words UNITED STATES OF AMERICA and on the other, E PLURIBUS UNUM. At the crack of the bullwhip, the troupe would parade out of the boxcar singing "Home on the Range."

From the beginning, it was a real crowd pleaser. It descended upon America like a chapter out of *Huckleberry Finn.* It was the reason many men first sat in a theater. It was Vermont maple syrup; the logs Abe Lincoln split.

It was everything we ever wanted to be. It was something to hand down to your children and your children's children.

It was a horny-nosed Western centipede with one hundred legs.

It would stop people on the street and show off its one hundred feet. The people would look at all those feet and open their mouths just like there was a first time for everything.

There's no business like show business.

After a while the people lost interest in the Wild West Show. They were tired of it. They wanted something new, not just more of the same.

And they would stay home and watch television when Buffalo Bill came to town. Bill wondered if it was P.T. Barnum who had said, "You could please some of the people some of the time, but none of the people all of the time." Man's heart away from nature was growing hard.

Reliving the old days in the West for those who had never been there was not enough. The long weary miles, the songs, the jokes, the dangers, the physical hardships, the cattle roundups, desperados, stagecoach holdups, burning wagon trains--it was just not enough.

Buffalo Bill wanted to out-Barnum Barnum, but all the fancy trick riding, Indian war dances, bronco busting, sharp-shooting, even his 1882 "Old Glory Blow Out" in North Platte on the Fourth of July, all this Western melodrama was just not enough.

The plots and backdrops of the real West began to seem thin, watered down. The life of the West crossed its own Great Divide, heroic and romantic, beyond men's wildest dreams. Somewhere inside them, men knew they were missing something and waited sadly for that vital force to come alive.

During these depressing years, Buffalo Bill used to go down to the Bowery and sit with all the bums, dangling their feet together over the East River. He would look over at the Statue of Liberty and remember his old friend Kit Carson's words about the buffalo. He stared at that lovely guardian of New York Harbor and thought of the new world she represented. And finally he thought, "The show must go on!"

But the Wild West Show must be more than entertainment, the mere winning of the West.

Bill looked down his hatchet nose and pulled on his buffalo-head goatee and wondered what was missing.

* * * *

Beyond the iron bars of his cage in the army garrison, the white buffalo could see the stars outlining the constellation of Taurus the bull, and further over in the night sky a hint of Orion the hunter. It was now the tenth year of the old bull's incarceration.

"You have hurt me, and later you will regret it," thought the white buffalo simply.

This remark was aimed at no one in particular, but in the face of the American flag flying over the fort, it only spurred on his pent-up feelings of hostility. Yes, for a long time he had been fooled into thinking he would be set free. Kind, young officers would stroll by his cage and pet him, gently and without fear. He had placed his trust in them like a nation that would free its slaves. Yes, and all for nothing. He had suffered all alone; yet in life isn't one always alone, he asked himself.

Exasperated, he turned his head away from the dark night and tried to sleep.

His dreams quickly carried him out West, to nothing but the land itself, whole and impenetrable. He saw himself grazing in the tall grass with strings attached. Each jerky step he took was awkward and puppet-like. A caricature of his true self, he dangled stiffly like a wooden marionette. Desperately he tried to erase this hideous image and replace it with a gentler one.

The wooden buffalo did not stir. What was he frightened of? He wanted to tell the dream animal that he was out of his mind, cruel, unfair, that he, the white buffalo alone, was true and real. But first he must come close enough to show his trust. Then they both would understand.

But, no, here he was instead, putting his face between the iron bars. The buffalo reached out two white hoofs and seized him by the hair: two long, black braids. He was determined to show his strength, and with his bloodshot eyes wide open now, he looked into the deep, brown ones of Sitting Bull.

Instantly his anger fell, as though he had struck a deadly blow. White as a sheet, the buffalo moved as close to his friend as the bars would allow. At first neither could speak.

"I must have been crazy! Did I hurt you?"

"I must talk to you..."

Then they laughed. The strange feeling of impotence and emptiness was gone. He no longer feared his dream and the world was again within his reach. In that brief moment the buffalo and the Indian committed yet one more small part of themselves to each other.

"My friend, what's the matter?...How did you get out?"

Sitting Bull said nothing, watching the moonlight on the buffalo's face. The sight of his pale brow saddened him.

"I heard your moans...and broke out," he said quietly, and he could find nothing further to add.

The white buffalo waited, but did not move. Trying to conceal his excitement, he asked in as calm a voice as he could muster:

"Will you make a run for it?"

And in his heart he knew they would both be running toward the open plains before dawn. Someone had turned the lights in the white house back on, and a voice was calling out in the fading night: "Quickly, we must go..."

Earlier Sitting Bull had stolen the keys to the white buffalo's cage from the sentry office. Now he hastily unlocked the door. The bull stepped out awkwardly, shaking his legs and stretching his back and hump to loosen up his limbs after their long confinement.

Behind his left shoulder he could feel time flowing by without injury. He looked at the Indian, standing tall beside him. Together, they would put all of this behind them, would rejoin their own lives again.

"Ten years...ten years...yet a lifetime! And we gave them everything we had to give..."

Cautiously they made their way to the edge of the fort.

The sun had not yet risen when the man and buffalo slipped past the entry guard and emerged into the breaking day like a morning star.

* * * *

In the empty grandstand of New York's Madison Square Garden, Buffalo Bill stared up at the banner hanging from the rafters:

BUFFALO BILL'S WILD WEST

&

CONGRESS OF ROUGH RIDERS OF THE WORLD

His partner, the notorious sharpshooter Dr. W.F. Carver, sat beside him puffing on an expensive Havana cigar. It was as dark inside the arena as the hour before dawn. It would be daylight soon, and the two had been sitting there all night, since the close of last evening's performance, discussing the declining box office receipts.

"Strike a match," Bill said. "At least that will give us a little light." Dr. Carver lit up his cigar again, and blew smoky circles out into the vast, dark hall. For a moment, things seemed a little brighter.

"I wish you'd come up with something," Bill scolded himself. He stood up and stretched his legs, which were cramped inside his shiny-black, hip high boots. Stylish, but impractical.

There he stood, Colonel William Cody, the determined and serious showman, and what he had once been, the fearless and experienced guide, scout, frontiersman, and Indian fighter, standing slightly bent in his tight boots, a tremendous Stetson tipped roguishly to one side of his proud head.

He who had made the show; he who had actually lived the life unfolding before the Wild West spectators;

he who drew the crowds; it was his presence that made it real, and yet somehow unreal at the same time. The star attraction, whose image penetrated the American mind, was overbearing, sensational, too much. What they needed now was not something that only dramatized the West, outlined it like a silhouette, but an offering of its living spirit, vital and thrilling.

"I wonder," Dr. Carver mused aloud, "if the folks might not like to see a real, live buffalo. Something wild and a bit terrifying might draw them back."

In the hazy drift of cigar smoke, Bill thought of the powerful animal with the muscular torso and solid frame. That wondrous hump. The untamable animal, which above all characterized the Wild West. He pictured his shaggy head with diamond eyes, a trophy in his life. And then Bill's own eyes suddenly rang up like a cash register.

"That's it, that's it!" he kept repeating, as he pulled Dr. Carver up from his seat, and ran with him out of the Gardens and into the city that was now flooded with morning light. His own voice sounded like an echo of itself and bounced against the tall buildings as if it meant business. "Yell louder," Dr. Carver suggested. "Maybe someone will tell you where to find an old buffalo while you're at it!"

"They may all be gone out West, but I know where there's still one left. I left him there myself. But there's no time to talk. We may be too late as it is."

Dr. Carver took out a flask from his hip pocket, and lifted it in the direction of the Lady of New York Harbor. Grinning fatuously, the two men drank to the white buffalo.

15 The Bone Trail

A thousand miles west of New York an Indian and a buffalo looked at the morning after with bleary eyes. It was difficult to speak without cliches. The images that focused inside them were stirring up poignant memories. They lowered their heads as if to protect themselves from the intensity of those experiences. Instead, a signpost caused them to look up.

The Bone Trail: They were headed north out of Dodge, where they had spent the night, and were now wending their way up into North Dakota. On their way they bypassed several drivers of wagons, loaded with old bones. The men were all in a hurry, urging their horses on with their whips, as if these bones were as valuable as gold.

They met other men coming down the trail, each burdened with a sackful of bleached bones on his back.

Suddenly they were standing in front of a white mountain of bones, twelve feet high, twelve feet wide, and a half-mile long. It was a very strange cemetery and a kind of collection of trophies glaring like a death mask. Sitting Bull held a large, white femur to his ear and heard a roaring moan, more terrible than the whole ocean pounding in on him. Hastily he threw the bone back on the pile, and it tumbled over and over, clacking against vertebrates, ribs, wishbones, skulls, ulnas, sacrums, scapulas, tibias, the whole skeletal structure, until it finally came to rest at the white buffalo's hoofs.

There was a ladder leading to the top of the Buffalo Bone Business. Yankee Ingenuity was sitting on the top rung with his partner, a German chemist. They were grinding away at a capacity of thirty to fifty tons a day. Like everything else, they were in it for the money.

At the bottom of the ladder, the bone pickers were collecting, assorting, and mixing the refuse into common fertilizer phosphates. The good bones were used exclusively for refining sugar.

They overheard one bone picker tell another:

"The work is boring, but it's a damned easy way to make a buck."

The white buffalo was ashamed to look at this mountain of bones, exposed like a descecrated gravesite. Up until now the trail had been a game. He had no idea where it would lead. He whose steps were so sure had never wondered whose bones were being carried off on men's backs. Only now, for the first time, did he really see them.

He sank down into the dry grass at the bottom of the heap and looked back up. Bones, as far as the eye could see. He closed his eyes, as though this nightmare might disappear. Inside his mind forests, lakes, and plains whirled around him; yet each time he opened his eyes, the ghostly mountain was there before him.

"What do you think of our bone business?" someone was asking Sitting Bull.

The Indian looked about, not knowing what to say: this ladder seemed rickety, and the mountain lacked solidity. It might all come tumbling down at any minute.

The white buffalo, meanwhile, was amazed to see himself still alive. He checked just to make sure, pinching himself in the ribs. And he realized he could still hold himself up for a long time yet to come, like the solid frame of a house.

The very framework of the West was changing: those massive hills whose ridges were rooted in the earth, already they had been torn apart by gold diggers trying to get to the bottom of things, and finding nothing.

The Indian and the buffalo left the Buffalo Bone Business behind them, the dead leaves crackling underfoot. Neither one of them could speak. But in their hearts they knew that the spring would replenish the few buffalo that were left.

Now, after all this running, the buffalo knew the language of the dead and was not afraid of it. Each sacrificial carcass had added its own voice to the voice of the house. What would endure was the breath that would continue to speak, would never change. Even his limbs were now free to express themselves in his work.

He must try to believe this image he was offering himself and the remainder of the herd. He would seek this vulnerable left shoulder and bury his face in the refuge of his hump, like some wounded, wild animal preparing to die.

16 Wanted--Dead or Alive

When it dawned on Bill up there in the empty grandstands of Madison Square Garden that he should take the wildness of the buffalo and put it in the center of the ring, he forgot for a moment that the prospect of actually finding a buffalo on the plains was next to impossible.

Yes, there was that incredible white buffalo he had captured ten years back in the Sioux camp with Sitting Bull. But he was a very old bull even then, and the chances of finding him still alive were slim.

Bill and Dr. Carver came down from New York to Fort Leavenworth to procure the buffalo for the show. When they arrived, they found wanted posters with a photograph of the Indian and the buffalo tacked up on the bulletin board.

The words under the photos said:

> Wanted, Dead or Alive, a White Buffalo Bull and his faithful Indian companion, Sitting Bull. Presumed to be heavily armed and extremely dangerous. $1000 Reward for Information leading to their Arrest or Capture.

Bill had a sick feeling in his stomach. It was one of those moments which hold out no hope of there ever being another. He thought it was the world which was rotten, outside events which had turned against him. "How could they...," he began to argue with himself.

Immediately he realized they must have headed West, gone back home. He would find them before they could get there. He would ask the sentry when he had first noticed their absence and determine from that how far they would have run by now. He would then take a train, get ahead of them, and recapture them by surprise.

The faces on the wanted poster were looking at him with the grim determination of survivors.

"Those goddam fools...trying to find their way alone..." He worried about them as if they were already his property.

"Let's shove off!" Dr. Carver reminded him.

They walked down to the railroad station and caught the next train heading West.

Bill tried to calm himself by stroking his goatee, and he felt vaguely reassured.

Now he slept. Strange visions of a brown dustcloud descending on the prairie swept across his mind. A tremor of the heart. Quick, he must find himself where the rainbow arched close to the ground. The treasure he sought was nearby.

There the everlasting perseverance ended in success. The land itself rose into the sky. These mountains, with men's faces cut into their sides, cast a grim but steadfast shadow over the Black Hills.

The Indians and the buffalo watched yet another monument going up in the black-green forests of ponderosa pine. These towering granite spires that arose out of the last American wilderness bore white men's names: Washington, Lincoln, Jefferson, and Theodore Roosevelt. Names that did not roll easily off the tongue.

The buffalo, the Indians, the deer, elk, grouse, wild turkey, mountain goat, and the few black bear couldn't remember the intricate names and still called the place "Paha Sapa."

* * * *

Buffalo Bill Cody and Dr. Carver were creeping up a dimly lit trail in the scenic Black Hills of South Dakota.

They examined the fresh cloven hoofprints in the path and knew they were on the right track.

After running undercover from tree to tree for a thousand yards, they stole up the path in front of the two sleeping figures alongside the trail. It was dark. They quickly dropped a net over the pair on the ground, and then pulled it tight.

"What's going on?" Sitting Bull sat up abruptly with his eyes still half shut, while his hands flailed wildly in an effort to free himself from the net.

The commotion woke the white buffalo, and he was snorting and trying to paw his way out of the trap. The more he thrashed, the more entrapped he became.

The two men standing above them with their legs spread apart and their arms folded in a gesture of firm control, grinned at each other smugly.

There, at last, was the great white behemoth lying helpless on the ground. All they had to do now was wait for the railroad men they'd hired to catch up with them and carry the captives back to the waiting train. Colonel William F. Cody sighed with relief: the future was back in his hands.

* * * *

The sides of the boxcar were covered with large canvas broadsides advertising Buffalo Bill's Wild West Show. On one side was the larger-than-lifesize picture of the white buffalo and on the other, the image of Sitting Bull in full feathered regalia.

In St. Louis the train received much attention. By the time it reached Chicago, it was the talk of the town.

Thousands of the show's spectators from Chicago to New York City had never before seen a buffalo. They marveled at the animal's curious hump, at his cloven feet, at the untamable look in his eye, and the shining forehead. At the end of each performance the people walked away with tears in their eyes.

Weeks passed. Then months. And the box office receipts skyrocketed until they were out of sight.

In the first season, Cody had tried to have men rope and ride the buffalo. This proved too dangerous, and Bill could not even persuade Sitting Bull to sit on his friend's back. He could see that the Indian respected, but also feared, the buffalo's hump. Bill dismissed this as pure superstition.

Next, Cody tried out a spectacle showing a buffalo hunt, a difficult feat since the bull would turn on the men, lowering his head and pawing the ground as if he were about to charge. Finally the fearful trainers would have nothing more to do with the buffalo, and

Bill decided it was time to have a heart-to-heart talk with the old bull.

Now, Buffalo Bill Cody was a Piscean, and natives of this sign are highly emotional. It was all this emotion that made Bill speak to the buffalo as one human being to another. After all, Bill needed the bull's full cooperation in order to keep the show in the black. This is what he said to the white buffalo:

"You realize, don't you, that you're much better off here in the show than you could ever be back on the plains? Out there you'd be shot in no time at all! Nobody will hurt you while you're with me. Goddam it, you are a treasure; doesn't old Bill Cody know a good thing when he sees it?"

The white buffalo was his last chance. If not him, no one could save him. He had already tried Annie Oakley, Pawnee Bill, Calamity Jane, Geronimo, all the big names--to no avail. Even the Indian chief who made the nickel famous was not the old, reliable draw he once was. Only this wild animal could save them now. How could he make him understand, see how he needed him in this last desperate hour?

The white buffalo drew himself up to his full stature and looked at this man with the hatchet nose and buffalo-head goatee as if to tell him the answer was as obvious as the nose on his face.

Bill Cody looked back into the eyes of the powerful animal and again searched for an answer in those deep pools which seemed to have no bottom.

For a long time he had been perplexed by the world he had made for himself, that world which kept slipping away from him everytime he tried to hold on to it.

And suddenly he realized the insignificance of all he had so far had to face: nothing but a mimicry of real life, ten years amusing Americans and Europeans alike with his imitation of the West. In the buffalo's eyes he saw true experience. The people must have seen this too. Their tears were for the deep-rooted sense of place and self they felt in the animal's presence. It was against himself surely, his own being, that Cody had been struggling all these years. He was already maimed by what he had torn away from the living frontier.

He touched the buffalo very tentatively on that sacred hump, but realized the futility of this final gesture. He knew he must let him go.

The white buffalo waited like stone, his hump rising and falling in the silence that fell between them. He knew this man could not change, but perhaps a small branch had snapped inside him, allowing a token of understanding to spread through his body. He wanted to help the man in his apparent agony, but he had done everything he could: he shook his horns as if to say, "No blame." No, he blamed no one for anything, nothing anyone had ever done could alter history's solitary undertaking.

Where would he go now? How would he find the Black HIlls without a map or compass? Without being captured again? Although he was prepared for the desolation he would see on the road back, he was surprised at this detachment.

Around him the frontier kept up the same pointless hustle and bustle. Amid all this chaos he felt lost. Slowly he pushed on against this alien crowd, thinking to himself: "It's as though I weren't here." Soon he would be gone too, like the rest. His job, he knew, would tie him down for a while like the railroad pounding against the land. Although limited, his impact was still in the making. One day, he was wishing, his life would be as real as that iron horse steaming across the continent. It was curious, yet sure: it was not for himself he wished this, but for the others.

He knew that each day, step by step, was moving toward something new and disquieting, this vast territory was going away from where it had once been uninterrupted for centuries. Going back to the beginnings, the roots of things, and pursuing them to the end, he had come to know the lessons of birth and death--the union of seed and power that produces all living things. In this way, the white buffalo had come to resemble heaven and earth and his wisdom embraced all things. Although he had suffered--they had made him suffer--he rejoiced in his knowledge of fate and was therefore free.

A single dot wandered alone across the land, a white mass which the horizon quietly gathered in, enveloped in its peace, gentle as death.

* * * *

Lookout Mountain, Colorado is the town where William Cody went to die, and the town has a Buffalo Bill Museum. Anyone is welcome to go in and look around. Western bric-a-brac, his dirty white buckskins, string ties, a faded poster of Bill on his faithful horse Brigham, Lucretia Borgia with her butt polished to a high sheen are all here gathering legendary dust.

Lookout Mountain, Colorado is at the timberline, and you can see for miles and miles in all directions when you're standing on top. Some people think they can see the entire West from on top of Lookout Mountain.

Following a series of "Farewell Exhibitions," Buffalo Bill retired to Lookout Mountain, Colorado with $3 million dollars. He didn't want to, but his doctor told him to go home to die.

Everyday he would go up on top of that mountain and look out over the West, still seeking the treasure he never found, and then go into his museum and gaze at the 4,280 sets of buffalo horns mounted on the wall.

Peering into the exhibit cases, he wondered if anyone had ever done as much for his country.

There is a fully stuffed buffalo inside a glass case in the Buffalo Bill capital of America.

17 The West Wind

Someone had folded up the brown blanket and put it away. There was no sign of it anywhere.

The little row of cow towns that narrowed the West was a six-lane highway, up and down which the white buffalo ran, searching for the lost herd.

He watched the crowds rush by, and felt himself left behind by this ongoing flood. Each person hurrying somewhere, bent on some unknown purpose; plans set up and cancelled; out of time and out of place. Once this crowd had been a handful, and now it was like a Fourth of July parade, filled with bright pyrotechnics and shooting stars. Some of them, brightly colored and long-lasting, would help to heal the deep wounds in the Western landscape, while others would curl up and fizzle away like black charcoal snakes on the sidewalk.

A strong west wind was blowing dust into his eyes as the white buffalo tried to move against it.

I must walk quickly, he thought. Maybe he wouldn't have to travel much longer. But whether he found the herd or not, he would return to the Black Hills as soon as he could.

He was still a little confused by the changes he saw around him. Cities and towns had sprung up where once familiar Indian villages had stood. Fields of grain were growing on the old grazing lands. Even the once reliable trails had been replaced with these black macadam highways which were hard and long under his hoofs, accustomed to a more varied terrain.

He took a deep breath of the pine woods that blew against him, and held it in his nostrils like a friend.

The long highway hurried nowhere and had no end. It was the old Santa Fe Trail, but he no longer recognized it. Its speed and sense of urgency finally wearied him, and he turned off the highway at the next junction.

Everything was different now. He had slowed down enough to see things in a clearer perspective, and the wind had shifted, drying the stinging tears from his eyes.

Suddenly the land seemed utterly vast and lonesome, too big, too empty. It made him feel small and he wished he could recover his heart from his sleeve, out where everyone could see how he felt about things. He wanted to be quiet, anonymous. But everywhere he saw wheels rolling over the hills, people and plows. Movement.

When he was tired he would stop and watch men working in the fields. He watched the oxen, yoked and straining at the bit, with special interest. His heart pulled with them. The oxen driver saw the white buffalo out of the corner of his eye and sensed the change in the oxen's pace. When he looked over at the old bull, he had meant to holler something to chase him away, but instead he opened his mouth and stood there speechless.

Others who saw him thought they knew him, but they weren't sure. Buffalos had been gone for so long that the new generation on the plains and prairies knew them only by word-of-mouth from the oldtimers, and most of the time they thought the old gaffers were stretching things in their stories about the huge, shaggy, hump-backed, ferocious bison.

The buffalo began to avoid the little towns and farm settlements. He was always shocked by the sadness he provoked in those who saw him. Sometimes a band of high-spirited boys would chase him or try to rope his head, but he easily outran these youthful attempts at capture. He could see that their hearts were not really in it.

One man said to his wife, "That's a horse of a different color. Don't fool with him; he means business."

An old woman said to her grandson, "He reminds me of the house where I grew up."

But the buffalo who could no longer bear to see these people so disturbed by his presence, found an old trail and set off to look for the herd.

Until now the white buffalo had thought all the changes he had encountered in the West were outside himself. He saw the alterations like the land itself, at times calm and quiet, and at other times dark and violent as the unpredictable weather.

He wasn't sure when he had first noticed the change in himself, but one day he realized that even the shape of his body was different. He knew that his hump had grown, but the change in the rest of his body had not been so obvious.

Perhaps he would never have noticed if he hadn't seen himself in a full-length mirror he passed outside a general store in a rural village one morning. He was so startled that he walked back and took a second look.

He saw his reflection wearing a different coat and speaking with a different accent and supporting himself on a different frame.

He began to wonder if he were seeing things, when the child came out from inside his body and told him that everything was alright, he was still there just the same as he'd always been.

The white buffalo returned to the image in the mirror and saw himself running, all of these years moving back and forth across invisible borders, with the trigger pointed at his vulnerable left shoulder. He saw the piles of plush, brown robes, the stacks of tongues eaten as delicacies, the tenderloins in butcher shops, and that white mountain of bones. Everywhere he looked, he saw men's minds chalking up profits and inventing America.

In his mind he called his friends in. They looked at the reflection and all sickened at the sight. He held the mirror up so that each one could see what he had become. He called it "The Necessity of Invention."

In a matter of years the buffalo had evolved, proving how rapidly such specialization takes place. He had longer legs and a longer, lighter body now than the heavier buffalo of early years. During the last years he had been so constantly pursued and driven from place to place that he never had a chance to put on fat. As a result of this continual running, he had changed from a stocky, short-backed, short-legged animal to this new shape with long, speedy legs and a light, rangy body custom-made for running.

There was nothing the buffalo could not outrun. Not the horse, not men in their open wagons, not even the Union Pacific train rushing across one side of the continent to meet the other.

* * * *

It was less a small town railroad station than a last-ditch effort for an exotic adventure, a safari. A scenic excursion across the heartland of America. The stationmaster gave them each a brochure which outlined their journey:

THE WAY WEST
Points of Interest

1. Dodge City--The Cowboy Capital
2. The Far West Restaurant
3. The Old Santa Fe Trail
4. An Authentic Indian Reservation
5. The Slaughteryards of Kansas
6. The Continental Divide
7. Custer's Last Stand
8. The Buffalo Bone Business
9. The Necessity of Invention
10. The End of the Line

Three hundred people left Lawrence, Kansas on the Union Pacific Railway in a tour party organized for the benefit of a church. They had chartered the entire train, consisting of six passenger coaches, one smoking car, a baggage car, and a freight car. Altogether there were 30 women, 280 men, and 75 guns. They spent the first night playing faro, drinking whiskey, smoking, and sleeping on the hard wooden seats.

Everything was just as the attractive brochure had so eloquently said it would be: noble, savage, and utterly unique.

There wasn't anything like it anywhere else in the world.

Wilderness soon.

(Imagining, dreaming. Had it occurred to them, these pleasure seekers, that this might not be all fun and games?)

This scenic excursion, this trip into the future and the past, this expanding landscape, riding out history...

It will be wilderness soon.

Now they were weary, tired of the rattling train carrying them to the end of the line. They wanted to forget it all for a while in the luxury of sleep.

By midnight everyone wished they had thought to bring an extra blanket. Someone passed around some thin, brown Army blankets, and they pulled them up around their shoulders, but they weren't much use against the wind pushing through the cracks in the car.

The West was asleep at last. It had been a long, hard day and the buffalos waiting in the Black Hills needed their rest for tomorrow. It was here they had spent a dozen years waiting for the vision to reappear. That same night the little passenger train, the Union Pacific, would make possible the re-entry which brings reality back from the world of fairy tales.

And that night a traveler would return them to themselves. His white body would show up like a ghost of the past. But in the depths of his hump would be buried a memory impossible to ignore, a memory the shape of a blanket, wooly, thick, and brown, stretched now like a taut canvas about to explode into a rainbow of colors.

Nobody would be surprised. Nobody would jump at the cloven footsteps, coming nearer and nearer. Nobody would even gasp when the white house shone through the pines, welcoming them home. Now, all the lights in the house were flooding through the forest.

The white buffalo found his rosebud quilt where he'd left it at the foot of the bed. He was glad to be home in his own bed again, this rich spot of earth that remembered him.

In the morning a harsher light was embracing the world. Most of the herd were up early and bathing in the nearby river.

The lead bull had already sounded the morning bell that rang out against the sky like a branding-iron. The herd began to move back together for the parting words before they headed off for their final project.

The wind was coming from the west. Visibility was normal. No clouds. Everything was in order. Only the last words were left to be spoken.,

The guest speaker needed no introduction. As in a rush to catch the last train home, the white buffalo quickly came to the point.

The wind from the west blew up in his face.
He began:
"There's a smell of burning flesh out there. When the wind is right you can even smell it up here. We can no longer set our teeth in the thick grass without regret. Nor rub what does not belong to us."

The western wind was beginning to blow harder.

"It is time now to do what we must do. To show our strength. Not the strength of numbers that we once were, but the power that comes from endurance. We must settle back into the wonders that may never cease."

The wind, like an overcharged battery, kept building.

"Your humps are powerful now, like strong medicine. I am entrusting you to your own safekeeping."

Everything was silent except for the wind, which was furious.

"Do you know this song?"

He hummed the tune.

It was coming back to them, and they joined the high-pitched whistling of the wind.

It was time. They entered the plains like a brown dustcloud, flecked with gold.

Running, running.

18 A Brown Dustcloud

The great plains screeched to a halt. The buffalos ran across it with their tongues out and their heads down in a race for life. They puffed the wind in and out of their mouths. The young calves spanked themselves with their tails as they ran.

The ground spread out before them like a welcome mat.

Wheel ruts, buffalo trails, crosses left behind by unlucky wagon trains, scrub brush, a few lone pines, and broken arrows blurred together as they ran. Everything was taken up into the sky: a whirlwind the shape of a brown animal.

The stampede, passionate, single-minded, obsessed, at the height of emotion that was never meant to be released.

The sun passed aimlessly overhead. There were no shadows, everything glaring and bright.

Full speed ahead. On and on, covering more ground in a minute than a wagon in a morning.

There was no stopping them.

The buffalo were mad.

Incensed at their mistreatment, as if by plan they were on the rampage. Shoulder to shoulder, this great brown army came on with the courage of an undefeated clan, small in numbers, threatened, holding out their last card.

Thundering. The whole earth shook with the heavy hoof upon the ground.

It is not easy to kill a buffalo. His spirit is so fierce that his death throes blare like fire alarms. As they approached the Union Pacific train, they began to think with their humps. They slowed down, almost coming to a complete halt, growing tense in their shoulders at the thought of what lay ahead.

The passengers had asked for the West and received a bonus. But nothing in the brochure had prepared them for this. Somehow they had associated real danger, true experience, with the dark continent, the unexplored territories.

But, after all, this was America, where anything was possible.

They entered the final ritual, with a glowing white bull for a beacon, and the West began to recover its true dimensions. The train grew old seeking to reach its destination. Stalled, it had stuttered to a stop, belching black smoke. These plains, an hour ago, had been a place deprived of the past. There were new towns coming up like rows of freshly planted corn, and an army waiting for surrender, vague uprisings, an uneasy truce. But the bellow of a buffalo brought the plains to life, a roaring animal recreated the past, something born, running for its life, and reborn in another body.

Changed, the herd served as a measure of true distances. New proportions. The map must be reconstructed with simpler lines, intersecting and drawing sustenance from one another--the buffalo would once more be there to light the way.

What an eloquent morning! Already, how dazzling his presence seemed. The white buffalo, with a final gesture, swept his lowered head over the entire West.

A single dot filled the plains.

Somewhere, he sensed, a young calf was deserted by the death of his mother, and hope was slipping relentlessly beneath the dark, rich topsoil.

And now the iron horse and the buffalo met.

In a matter of seconds the herd had systematically surrounded the train, covering each car with their strong torsos and impaling the wooden sides with their shaggy heads and horns. The earth was trembling violently and the sound of thunder intensified. Inside the train each man cocked his rifle, found a good position, and began to fire.

At first they aimed above the animals' heads, hoping to frighten them away. The buffalo rifles were not meant for close range, and the men wanted to drive the herd back to a reasonable distance from the train where they could pick them off, one by one.

But the buffalos were not about to be scared off by a few harmless shots in the air. Together they pushed their bodies against the wooden cars until the strong timbers were splinters. Men, women, and baggage were now sitting in the open, unprotected. And then they began to attack the men themselves, ripping them apart like straw scarecrows. No, they would not be frightened away like so many cawing birds: this pecking, an invasion, was meant to last.

Eventually the men regained their senses. The thundering hoofs, the click and clatter of clashing horns, and the animals' bellowing had almost drowned out their reason, but the armed hunters now began to shoot point blank into the brown mass of flesh. The rush of buffalo immediately dispersed. Alarmed, the front line packed shoulder to shoulder, charged at anything in sight, leaping wildly into the cars and trampling everything underfoot. Panic mounted. Women screamed hysterically, some running straight into the oncoming buffalo and meeting their certain death.

The wounded began to fall. Hoofs splashed through pools of blood. The dead and dying, man and animal alike, were strewn everywhere, arms upon limbs, human hair blended with brown fur.

As buffalos dropped to the ground, those still standing began to bellow and paw the earth. Some moved from one downed animal to the next, sometimes butting the dead with their big, shaggy heads. Everywhere the treasure, that had glimmered briefly and gone unrecognized, staggered, rose up for a moment, then fell back to earth.

In the final act of retaliation the few buffalo still alive, although weakened and wounded, came together one more time and leaned their immense bodies against the wreckage of cars, tipping the Union Pacific over on its side, where it lay like a dying animal.

The storm was over. As if someone had yelled "fire," the panic-stricken men began rushing in every direction, and the buffalo galloped into the western wind that had brought them to this conclusion.

The men stopped firing and walked around the crumpled train to witness the end of the line. They counted 120 dead buffalo, as many dead men, and numerous crippled on both sides.

Was it here the West ended, in rubble, in distress, with no witness? Was it here the tangible world opened on fantasy where nothing is ever real? The little train that held so much promise of adventure, a connection to the land, was lost. The little train that thought it could, and pushed on into the wilderness by sheer will power, could not...

> *Joe, Joe, broke his toe,*
> *Riding on a buffalo.*
>
> *When he came back,*
> *He broke his back,*
> *Riding on a railroad track.*

Evening. For a time the white buffalo stumbled along as if an awful noise would overtake him, a holocaust. Then the heavy bleeding in his chest caused him to stop where he was and rest. Crouched in a fist, he wrapped his limbs around him like a blanket. Thunder and rain set in, the image of deliverance. The blood washed slowly down his chest and spilled on the ground around him. He knew it was another beginning, this scarlet blood that soaked into the land: it pardoned mistakes and forgave misdeeds.

He knew the work of deliverance must be carried through oneself; he knew this as he concentrated the medicine bundle on his shoulder upon the remembered earth. Upon this brilliant rainbow breaking into its prism of separate colors. He gave himself up to this particular landscape, looking at it from every possible angle. Again he knew the ponderosa pines, the Black Hills, that home on the range where the herd would somehow survive, and the treasure of every living thing. That shaggy white brow, those eyes with the deep unfathomable pools, the open mouth chanting its own death song saw everything as he passed into history.

   It was a good day to die.